Also by Naz Kutub

The Loophole

NAZ KUTUB

BLOOMSBURY

NEW YORK   LONDON   OXFORD   NEW DELHI   SYDNEY

BLOOMSBURY YA
Bloomsbury Publishing Inc., part of Bloomsbury Publishing Plc
1385 Broadway, New York, NY 10018

BLOOMSBURY and the Diana logo are trademarks of Bloomsbury Publishing Plc

First published in the United States of America in February 2024 by Bloomsbury YA

Bloomsbury books may be purchased for business or promotional use. For information on
bulk purchases please contact Macmillan Corporate and Premium Sales Department at
specialmarkets@macmillan.com

Library of Congress Cataloging-in-Publication Data
Names: Kutub, Naz, author.
Title: No time like now / by Naz Kutub.
Description: New York : Bloomsbury Children's Books, 2024.
Summary: Possessed with the ability to grant others extra time in their lives, when
seventeen-year-old Hazeem gives away more time than he has left to live, he grapples with
the consequences as he tries to reclaim those years and rediscover the true value of living.
Identifiers: LCCN 2023034757 (print) | LCCN 2023034758 (e-book)
ISBN 978-1-5476-0928-4 (hardcover) • ISBN 978-1-5476-0939-0 (e-book)
Subjects: CYAC: Time—Fiction. | Interpersonal relations—Fiction. | Gay people—Fiction. |
Fantasy—Fiction. | LCGFT: Fantasy fiction. | Novels.
Classification: LCC PZ7.1.K898 No 2024 (print) | LCC PZ7.1.K898 (e-book)
LC record available at https://lccn.loc.gov/2023034757

Book design by John Candell
Typeset by Westchester Publishing Services
Printed and bound in the U.S.A.
2 4 6 8 10 9 7 5 3 1

To find out more about our authors and books visit www.bloomsbury.com
and sign up for our newsletters.

To my sister:
thank you for loving me so

CHAPTER ONE

Time is the enemy.

How do I explain this? To me, time is made up of numbers, so maybe I'll start with a very big one: 31,536,000.

That's approximately how many times my heart has beat in the past year, and at an average of sixty beats per minute, according to the stethoscope app on my phone.

31,536,000 heartbeats making up 365 days. The entire year I've had to live without my dad.

And I've got roughly 692,800,000 beats left, if I live as long as he did.

But I'm still here, in my tiny room, perched at the edge of my bed, my phone glued just over my chest, the app amplifying the rhythm of my heartbeat through its speakers.

pum-pum pum-pum pum-pum

The steadiness of it at rest is a wonder. Also, miraculous that I'm at sixty BPM seeing how I have not done a single second of cardio this entire year.

Beats per minute. Funny how everything has to sync to a rule of time. Except that, as I was saying, time is my biggest enemy, and everyone else's, which I don't think anyone realizes.

The sound of my heart is entrancing, hypnotizing me, a signal that this meat battery has been installed to keep the bones and flesh of my body running, so I can pursue what I want to even if there's not a lot of pursuing to do.

With a sigh, I hop off the bed and hover by the window, just next to my hamster's palace, staring at the snow-white Mary Shelley who is fast asleep in her wheel. This whole complex of hers is a palatial construct I've assembled, occupying an entire corner of my room with four intertwining and labyrinthine floors of clear, multi-colored acrylic tunnels. All for her tiny paws to wander through every day.

I hope I keep her entertained, seeing how she's one of the last few lights still shining brightly in my life.

For a second, a moment of peace cloaks me because here I am, speared by the morning rays, trying to change up my daily routine.

Because today is the day. My dad's one-year deathiversary. And I'm just hoping the one person who I want with me at the cemetery can make an appearance, although it may be a bit of an undertaking. I mean, I'll obviously be going with my nana. But it'd be nice to have a third.

The app beeps faster. My heart rate spikes to seventy-four BPM. I try to calm myself down, trying to recall the teaching that

I've learned over the past year, the recollection of it slinging an arrow of guilt into my gut.

But after five . . .

four . . .

three . . .

two . . .

one . . .

deep breaths, I'm back down to sixty BPM.

It is my goal to keep my heart rate at that round number, because any lower and I may just be dead. Even if I'm already zombieing through each day with draggy feet, trying to figure out what the rest of this existence is supposed to look like.

But just before I get too deep in my thoughts, a chittering interrupts me. A pair of beady eyes suddenly stares at me from her palace. And there she is, my Mary Shelley.

"Oh, I didn't know you were up already," I say.

She looks around as if she's waiting for something. *Feed me already, dammit.*

"God, relax, you little rodent you. So demanding when you're hungry." I grab a baby carrot from a bowl on my nightstand, which I keep just for her, then I reach through the cage, surrendering it.

She grabs it with gusto, as if she's starving after having slept the entire night, the reverse-hibernating creature that she is. Hamsters are supposed to be nocturnal, but she's clearly adapted to my ways. Especially since she's outlived her own lifespan by an entire year. An anomaly no one has ever pointed out yet.

She's showing her age now, with that silky white fur, when it used to be a milky chocolate. But her eyes are still alert and she doesn't look like she's ready to give way anytime soon. Which I'm seriously grateful for, hoping she'll be able to stay with me for as long as possible.

As I reach in through the top of the enclosure and stroke her lightly on the head, the creaking swing of an opening door screeches my brain to a halt, followed by footsteps marching through the hallway past my locked bedroom door and down the stairs.

The stethoscope app instantly peaks to an eighty-four. Did not expect it to jump like that. But I guess I shouldn't be too surprised, considering the monumental task facing me in a few minutes. Confronting the one person I've no clue how to have a proper conversation with.

Today's the day it needs to happen. I need help to get to the cemetery. And I need to make sure that message gets across and that there's no way out of it.

So with my fingers crossed, I grab Mary Shelley out of her palace and situate her in her clear bubble dome backpack—which sits on my desk.

"Please please please be my emotional support today," I say.

She stares up at me as if to say she's up for the job. Or that it's pathetic a seventeen-year-old needs his hamster for emotional support.

I choose to believe it's the first one and toss the rest of the dozen or so sticks of baby carrots into the side pocket for her to snack on later.

With Mary Shelley's backpack slung over my shoulder, I make my way to the door and swing it open.

Inhaling a quick breath.

Into the hallway. Down the stairs.

Knowing that it's going to take every single ounce of my will-power to make a tiny request from the one person who doesn't give a damn about me.

My mom.

CHAPTER TWO

We live in a two-story house. One that looks pretty modern, with concrete walls outside and in. I think the style is called brutalism, which sometimes makes me wonder if it's meant to be taken literally. I mean, all the angular hard edges that I try my best to stay away from. Pretty sure they're razor sharp and can cut and draw blood from even the most innocent of skating gazes and glances.

And the inside of this house, to the observer who dares to scrutinize our living arrangements, may possibly reek of pretentious minimalism.

Because it pretty much does. Seriously, the place is so bare it should be labeled Unfurnished.

But it's not exactly . . . by design.

As I tread lightly down the stairs, I take in the white leather couch, the white credenza that houses a hidden flat-screen against that one white wall (silly me—all the walls are a stark, absolutely naked white), and that one white coat rack by the white door. It's obvious my mom is against the idea of a living room being for the living. Or for actually living in.

Because only ghosts live in here, I guess? Including the barely visible floaty thing that is me?

Maybe this style should be called accidental minimalism, but only because my mom had slowly and deliberately initiated a removal of all the Dad-ly things a week after he died. As in, she'd first taken one of his super vibrant watercolor paintings off the wall—and kept doing it on the daily, as she'd stare at one with a frown and a tear sliding down her cheek, putting each into hiding, or maybe storage, in his study at the far end of the lower floor of the house. The one room neither of us has set foot into since the clearing out had ended.

The rest of his things scattered throughout the house have gone into boxes that now hide in the rafters of the garage. Not a razor or a monogrammed hand towel or a man's shirt to be found.

He's been erased from existence in this place where I'm supposed to continue existing.

Now this whole house feels underbaked. Thanks to a few cups of my mom's monochromaticness, a few tablespoonfuls of flavorlessness, a few dashes of insouciance, and a few sprinkles of ennui. She's not the kind of person who desires decoration, or a change in furnishings. Which matches her straight-up, brain surgeon personality well.

And so, the bareness stands.

I tiptoe to the kitchen from the bottom of the stairs and hover in the threshold with Mary Shelley's bubble dome backpack behind me. "Need help with breakfast?"

The sudden voice in the still quietness of our morning startles the anxiousness that is Halimah, my mom. She winds through the kitchen cabinets with her back to me, her shoulder-length jet-black hair swaying all around as she sidesteps right, right, right, yet she doesn't bother turning to face the voice addressing her. "Do you know where the granola is? The French vanilla one? I had a sudden craving for it."

She'd go hungry if I wasn't around. This is our daily deal, with her needing help at sustenance. I've even taken over the grocery shopping most weeks. She's already lost twenty pounds in the past year, leaving behind brown skin that looks almost as translucent as rice paper, hanging on a mobile rack of skull and bones.

I settle Mary Shelley's backpack on the floor next to the kitchen island, then disappear into the pantry, reappearing with the sealed box of her favorite granola, sliding it across to her. "Want some milk?"

She grabs the box and stares at the nutritional content, really eyeing it, as if every extra gram and milligram value on the side may leech very precious brainpower she needs for her working day. "What do we have?"

To the fridge I go, to pull out a carton of oat milk, handing it to her. "This is what I got for us. It's all the rage in school and everywhere. A little pricey, though. Might be cheaper to make, so I can give that a try next time?"

What kind of desperate conversation is this coming from me? I have no desire to make oat milk. Ever.

My mom switches her gaze to the carton in her hand. "This is what everyone at the hospital is drinking right now, too. But you've got no time to do something as silly as actually making it. We're doing okay; we can afford it premade," says my highly privileged mom, as she grabs a bowl and spoon from the drying rack and settles herself at a barstool on the opposite end of the island. She pours a half cupful of granola into the bowl, then drowns it with the faux milk.

And then, she's just munching to herself, with her mouth closed. Eyes drilling deep down at her bowl, as if it's a patient's head she has to do surgery on.

But the granola is a deafening crunch in the five-foot chasm between us, the sweetness of vanilla puffing up cloying fumes into the air.

I'm here, at the other end of a sea of white marble, but I may as well be a million miles away.

All she has to do is move her pupils up half an inch, and she'll see me. But that won't happen.

Every morning, our ritual is one like this, of her scatterbrainedness and my helping guide her through it. She's been like this for the entirety of the past year.

I don't think she's meant it in any malicious way. Nana tells me grief changes people, and I get that. It's changed me, too. But is it weird that I've been forced to care for myself, to have to do all the adulting—for us—on my own, without any help from the woman who birthed and raised me?

Then again, she can't even care for her own well-being.

If a diamond was an actual person, it'd be my mom—unbelievably hard, with everything outside so shiny and distracting, to prevent you from seeing inside.

My mom can dress herself and make her entire person look presentable. She is a neurosurgeon, after all. The consummate pro at making her brain look like it functions well, so she can be allowed to continue to operate on the brains of others.

But the weirdest thing? Well, it has to be her unwillingness to even throw a casual glance my way. Not even a millisecond's worth.

So here I am, hanging out with the mother I've known my entire life, having to put up with how much the sight of my face causes hers to cleave with hurt.

She doesn't hide the flinch, or the grimace, when her eyes sometimes meet mine.

A lock of her hair strays from its immaculateness, and she tucks it behind an ear, as she continues to chew, swallow, chew, swallow, scrolling through a phone ding-ding-dinging with messages. "Oh God, these people at the hospital just won't leave me alone. Hazeem, what's on the schedule for today?"

I've been dreading having to reveal the most important day in my short life. "I think you . . . I . . . we were . . . are . . . planning to take Nana to the cemetery?" A quick pause after that shaky stumble of a sentence, before I find actual steel to wire my voice with. "You know, because it's the one-year anniversary of dad's death?"

The spoon in her hand freezes and her whole body seems to be stuck, as if the machine inside has become rusted from years of operating without grease, and it suddenly doesn't know which direction it should move.

Three seconds later, the cogs and gears start to spin again, and she springs back to life. "Oh," is all she says, as she resumes the process of masticating and consuming. "I've got to attend to some admin stuff. And then maybe I'll meet you two?"

My nod is exaggerated, dipping my entire head, not that she can see it. "Of course. Whenever you can make it, then." But my voice is calm, because it has to be.

I can't let her see the arrow sticking out of my side, an arrow she'd loosed with her indifference.

Then she gets up and shuffles her way to the sink to drop off the bowl, before dashing through to the living room. She grabs her bunch of keys from the stand next to the door, and says, "I'll check in with your nana later."

Then, she whooshes out to the garage.

The vroom of her Mercedes SUV floods through the entire house.

This whole place is huge. Two stories, three bedrooms.

And just one living(ish) person in it right now.

I don't think anyone knows how alone you are until you hear an echo, because that's when you realize what emptiness feels like.

And this house has been empty since the day my dad died.

But maybe an echo is the ghost of someone who used to live in it. Maybe it's him, trying to communicate with me.

If I listen carefully, I can hear his last words to me:

Count not the years.

I've always stopped myself from getting too far into deciphering its meaning, because I can't let four measly words dictate the rest of my life.

I'll never get a chance to ask Dad what he meant. Or what it's got to do with me.

Unless I can travel back in time. Which, I know, goes against every law of science and nature.

Yet sometimes, I can't help but wish.

CHAPTER THREE

There's that saying: "'Tis better to have loved and lost, than never to have loved at all."

My current mantra may just be: "'Tis better to have almost nothing, than to just keep losing."

Simpler, huh?

Anyway, I just can't figure out why my brain is such a jumble right now. And I can't easily make up my mind about anything. The one thing I do know is that I've got to get going.

I stick the bubble dome backpack—with Mary Shelley in it—on a side table, in front of the "living room" window, along with a full water bottle. And I make sure that the blinds are drawn slightly so that the sun is not coming down on her. This way, she gets to see everything outside.

And sadly, the one view we have is of the house that I no longer get to visit.

Yeah, that's Holly's house across the street. The one that looks like it's in utter disrepair. With its drooping eaves and the ivy climbing up the walls, and the red front door that's chipping paint.

We used to be the best of friends. And now we're not anymore. Something I try not to dwell on, because what's the damn point?

As Mary Shelley gets situated, I can't help but notice a shadow hovering in the bedroom window across the street.

There she is. Holly. I can tell because the shadow of her crutches is visible, too.

Her accident happened just a few short months after my dad died. There was no way I could have stopped it—I know that, after months of replaying it over and over and over again in my head—which made me wonder if she blamed me for it. And if that was why she'd stopped talking to me, and why we haven't spoken since?

A sigh erupts out of my lungs. "I wish Holly would just talk to me."

Mary Shelley just stares out the window, fixated on a squirrel climbing up a tree on the sidewalk. But then she turns to me as if to say, *Well, maybe you haven't tried hard enough.*

"I feel like I have. There is only so much I can do, you know."

She seems to wink. *I think you're being too hard on yourself.*

"Ah, there you go. I was just thinking that I was being too difficult about everything."

I won't say difficult. She's cleaning her paws now. *I think you just talk too much.*

"How dare you?" I say. "I've done my best to be your best friend. And here you go. Making fun of me."

14

Well, I hear you've got a long day. She's moved on to licking her nails. *Why don't you just go on and get out of here. It's nap time for me.*

"When is it not?" It's hard to not roll my eyes at her, until I remind myself that she's a hamster.

Don't forget I'm three years old. That's pretty much fifty percent older than I'm supposed to be.

"But I'm glad you're still around a little while longer."

Yeah, yeah, me too. She starts to yawn. *All right. Go along now.*

I do this more than I'd like to admit—having conversations with Mary Shelley, making up her voice in my head. But I had to find a way to fill the silence over the past year somehow.

But I do hope Nana is ready. I don't know if I'm going to be the best companion for her today, but I'll try my darndest.

In the garage, I'm about to step into the driver's seat of my two-door Mini Cooper when I catch a glimpse of the library book that's been in the backseat for the past year. Ugh, maybe it's time to finally take it back. Wonder what the fine on that's going to be.

Maybe I should punctuate this year with an actual period, and return it.

Do I have to?

Yes, I have to.

Let's just hope I can stop being a coward for five minutes to get the job done.

CHAPTER FOUR

My forefinger's tap-tap-tapping on the steering wheel. And all I can do is sit here, parked on the street, while staring at the entrance to the Burbank Library.

Yes, I am a coward.

My eyes rove all across the scene, while my free hand grasps tightly on the book loan that I have to return. It's about some kid who goes on a journey around the world with a maybe-magical genie, to go on a search for his ex-boyfriend, who's suddenly gone missing. I'd gotten to the part where he's about to board the genie's private jet and leave his ordinary world behind, but then the tragedy of my dad struck the very next day.

I also stopped reading because I got a little envious of the protagonist, for having a boyfriend at my age. When I desperately can't at seventeen . . . ugh, never mind.

So in my car it stayed, and now I really do have to return it; it's been an entire year and I don't know if I can continue the story where I left off.

Especially since I'm barely able to keep my own life story from derailing.

Outside, the birds are a-chirping somewhere up in those gigantic trees, and the squirrels are busy a-squirreling away their stolen nuts. And the cars zoom back and forth on the boulevard. And the pine trees are oozing their crisp scent.

Over the past year, moments like these always stand out to me. How the whole world can keep moving onward when mine has been slammed upside down. A weird side effect of grief that I've yet to shake.

I guess I really should just go ahead and make my way out of my car and into the library. Still, my legs don't move.

"They're probably not even here," I tell myself out loud, trying to sound somewhat convincing.

Okay, I'm doing it. Dammit, why's my heart spiking so hard right now?

I'm at a near-scramble, making my way over to the stout tan building. Wary of anyone about to approach or exit because I just don't think I should be anywhere near Yamany right now.

Since they'd told me they didn't want to see me ever again after I'd betrayed their trust.

My body flinches at the memory. Everything was great between us until I poked my nose into their personal stuff, and things just have not been the same again. Well, really, things just weren't . . . things anymore. Just like Holly, Yamany was one of the few friends I had who'd decided that they didn't want to be my friend at all.

And so with the book tucked into my arm, I dart through the door as it swishes open at sensing me, and I'm about to drop the book off into the gaping open mouth of the book drop bin when I see them.

Their intensely bright green eyes looking up from the computer screen, lasery and burning a hole through me from behind the counter as they realize who they're staring at, while twirling a fountain pen.

As if I've committed a murder and I've got the still-dripping knife in my hand.

All I can do is wave a finger at them. Yet some part of me wants to give a compliment about the cute floral blouse they have on, and tell them having their long hair bunned up like that makes their cheekbones pop.

But my feet won't move and my tongue's got a sudden injection of lead. It's as if the almost yearlong lack of our friendship hangs in the balance between us, the twenty feet feeling like a light-year's worth of distance, with them behind the counter and me just preventing the sliding glass door from closing as the air conditioning from the inside and the heat from the outside clash into me halfway. As if I'm torn between hot and cold.

Just like I'm torn by their super accusatory gaze, which reminds me of a scene in the beginning of that book where their best friend complained about being abandoned by the main character. Granted, they did eventually make up a few chapters later, so hopefully one day Yamany and I will make nice and patch things up. Because it doesn't seem like today is that day.

Yet I'm still compelled to stay. My eyes pleading even as my whole body starts to shudder.

Swish-clash-krrk goes the glass sliding doors.

But all Yamany does is turn back to the computer and spark a conversation with their coworker, who's intensely staring at a bunch of messy picture books on a rolling cart. Yup, a clear message that they're ignoring my presence.

I don't know if I'm deserving of being treated like this, but there's nothing I can do or say.

I did intrude that day. But it was only because I was worried. And I can only hope that they can forgive me someday, because right now I feel worse than a baby deer trapped between an alligator's mouth and the frozen ocean, and there's just no way anyone or anything can make me feel better about it.

My throat is closing up even as I reverse my way out, getting closer to my car. And as I stumble back, I finally do a lateral one-eighty, kind of glad that I was able to make it out of that non-exchange unscathed because I'm sure it could've gone a lot worse.

But still. It almost feels as if the entire universe has ganged up on me. And on today of all days. It's bad enough I lost my dad and multiple close friends in a year, and now it's like the universe is conspiring to reopen those wounds.

I'm nearly hyperventilating by the time I get back in my Mini, when a call comes through. No one calls me, except for the one person. I take a deep breath before answering. "What's up, Nana?"

"Hazeem," says the crackly voice, thick with age. "How far are you?"

"I had to drop something off at the library. On my way now."

"Make it ten. You are slower than I am. And I'm nineteen times your age."

19

She kills the line before I can say anything. But that's my nana. Her mantra seems to be: "There's always someplace to go instead of sitting around."

Totally at odds with mine. Because I'm fine with lying around, doing nothing.

For dayssssssssssssss . . .

CHAPTER FIVE

Nana? Are you ready?"

My voice booms through the house I've known since my baby-dom. The one that's always smelled like oud, her most favorite scent ever, a calming aroma that fills every nook and cranny, which is also stuffed with knickknacks of her past. Including a wall's worth of photos right next to her sixty-inch flat-screen that's usually got some classic Bollywood playing.

Where our house is severely lacking in everything, Nana's is all about excess.

And there she is, the queen of her domain. Perched on her couch in her favorite green dress. Arms crossed in front of her chest. Somewhat dampish short hair falling down to her neckline. "How long do you think I've been waiting, Hazeem?" she says. "Three hours."

My eyes want to roll themselves so bad, but she'll lunge at me to gouge them out at my insolence. "Nana, why are you exaggerating? Your hair is obviously still not dry. You've literally just taken a shower," I say, as I grab a headscarf from the coatrack by the door and make my way to her.

She looks at me sternly as she tries to get to her feet but stumbles a little. Nana is fiercely independent and refuses help for most things, even at her age, as an incoherent mumble-grumble rumbles out of her.

I can only hold out a hand. "It's okay to ask for help, Nana," I remind her for the millionth time.

She lets out a sigh as she clings on with both hands to my offering and heaves herself up to a standing position. And here she is in front of me. Her whole face lined with creases from decades of having to worry for us, for our family. For her family.

And after having lost her only child a year ago. "How are you, my boy?" she asks.

Nothing that a lie can't hide. "Better every day, I guess?"

Standing a whole head taller, I easily reach out and float the scarf over her before pinning it together below her chin the way she likes to wear it, while tucking in stray strands of gray hair.

"You don't have to do this for me all the time," she says.

Which is a lie. I know she enjoys it. But it's one of the few things I still feel like doing—just hanging out with her. Each passing second bleeds whatever life I have out of me, and it's only Nana—and Mary Shelley, of course—who reinvigorate me just a little. I'll never tell her that fact, but I have a feeling she can sense that my core is almost hollow.

I may just be a walking piece of skin. With eyes. And hair. And fingernails. But seriously, it feels like there's almost nothing left on the inside.

It's hard not to notice the smudge underneath her right eye. So I wipe away the excess kohl that she'd overapplied. "Nana, are you putting on makeup without looking in the mirror?"

"I know what I'm doing, silly boy. Your nana's been beautiful for the last sixty years," she says, with a swat at my forearm.

My fingers are all sticky now. "Well, look at this. Look at what I'm doing having to wipe all of this away."

"Why are you complaining so much? Aren't you glad your nana is here, always free enough to hang out with you?"

"Hang out? When did you start saying that?"

"I'm not that old. I know how to say the things that you young brats say."

She knows how I'm easily entertained by her antics, because to her, I'm absolutely *not cool*. Seriously, her words. Just because I stay home all the time now. And maybe she's in denial about me. But that's how she is. She's an overworrier, worrying about us all the time.

I guide her to the mirror by the entrance so she can add the finishing touches all on her own, then make my way into the kitchen to pack us some snacks and bottled water for the road. Because who knows what the day will have in store for us.

Gosh. I can't help thinking about my dad, when he used to be here, doing all this with Nana. Back then, back when he was alive, even just over a year ago, I'd whine at having to come over here even for a single minute. Because I wanted to be with my friends, since they were obviously more fun. Having to fuss over my very old and naggy grandma, making sure she took her meds and didn't leave a candle on, was such a bother.

Yet he never reprimanded me once for my selfish impatience. *Your nana loves you very much, and seeing you always brings her joy*, was what he'd say.

But what was always weird to me was how my nana would always act—as if she hadn't seen her grown ass son for years, when it could've been as recent as the day before. She'd inspect his face, comment on his lush mustache, the new grays growing out the sides of his head, and sometimes, cryptically mention the tinge of sadness that clouded his eyes.

There'd be some casual mention of her dead husband's terribleness, but my dad would simply change the subject.

He'd never say anything was wrong. I don't think he knew his health was in trouble. And I was too self-absorbed to even care to notice.

Ugh.

Anyway, I guess we're about to head out to see him.

I don't remember what his grave looks like. I was there once a whole year ago and I haven't been back since, even though Nana has been wanting to make a return visit the entire time. I just can't imagine having to visit any more than I have to. Knowing that my dad is buried underground. Reminding me that he's gone forever.

Everything we need goes into a tote bag, and now we're ready to go. But I find Nana rummaging through the drawers in the cabinet in the hallway. "What are you looking for?"

"My tiny Koran."

I riffle through the cabinet drawers and find a pocket-size one.

She grabs it and stuffs it into her pocketbook. "So are you ready, my dear boy?"

I don't know if I know how to answer that question. Even though her eyes are set with a determination that we will achieve something today.

Maybe closure?

All I know is it's going to be rough, and I'm hoping I'll be able to get through it without feeling entirely drained, my soul sucked dry, leaving behind a useless leathery thing with my face on it. It's true that my brain is heavily jumbled right now. But there's nothing more I can do other than to keep going, because Nana wants me to.

"I'm guessing your mom's not coming?" she asks.

My wince surprises even me, as I recall how she reacted this morning when I brought it up. "Well, she would have been in here with me already fetching you. But she's not here, is she?"

"Normally I would've spanked your smart mouth, but . . . not today." She gives me a nod almost as if she's been expecting it. "I guess it's just the two of us. Hazeem, your mom? Try to be understanding. She's going through things."

"I know, Nana. I know. But we all are, aren't we?"

Nana gives me a sad, almost pitying look. "But look at you. I'm proud of you for being this strong boy. Every single day."

Am I strong? I don't know if I am because every part of me is screaming—for love, for help, for attention, for more than I can name, even as I—

"Why are we still here?" she asks.

Oh Nana. Always the impatient one. "We're going."

"Yes, finally. Just have to stop and get flowers first."

"Okay, so after that, we're going."

She holds on to my hand. We make our way out.

And we can hopefully get this over with.

As fast as we can.

CHAPTER SIX

The closest place I can think of to get flowers is the grocery store five minutes from Nana's.

And as luck would have it, they've got a stand set up right outside, with some guy in a baseball hat spraying away at all the plants.

I park my car in the open lot as Nana tries to push me out to hurry me up.

Over at the stand, my florally clueless self stares at the tens of colorful bunches staring right back at me, and the guy's got his back to me, and he looks kinda busy, so I grab a bouquet of the brightest-looking ones I see, but then I second-guess myself, because what the heck do you get for a deathiversary? Are these *too* happy? Should I pick something more somber? Maybe he'll know if they have any black flowers or something equally dark.

Ugh. A groan escapes me as I make my way to the guy drowning all the blooms with many spritzes from a bottle. Maybe he'll know.

I work up the courage. "Excuse me, sir, do you know what . . ."

But the words melt on my lips like snowflakes on my skin as he turns around and stares at me. Because it's him.

Jack.

With those gigantic brown eyes that stare so deeply, and that neatly shaved head that's hidden underneath a baseball hat, plus that lean body with the swimmer's shoulders that's always left an oversized T-shirt hanging off it in just the right way.

But it's always that face. That jawline and that sharp nose. As if he belongs on a poster. A smoldery poster that will burn a hole in the wall that's lucky enough to be covered by it. Must be the Yemeni genes, all of which I can't seem to get enough of.

I think the right word to describe me in this scenario is "flabberghosted," because I'm super flabbergasted and the English dictionary has successfully and unequivocally ghosted me.

"Hey. What're you doing here?" he asks with a smile that lacks a twinkle.

Followed by no words. Just utter silence. Between us. A silence that stretcccccccchhhhheeesssss . . .

To the point where he gives up trying to be nice, wiping the smile off his face. "Sooooo . . . just the flowers?"

"I . . . I . . . I . . ." What in the wordlish word of wordling words . . .

Get a damn grip, Hazeem. You can do this. It's not every day that the boy you used to be in love with is standing in front of you at the grocery store that he obviously just started working at, and which you can never, ever visit again. "When . . . you . . . here?"

His eyes are suddenly filled with alarm, round as they are. "When did I start here? Three months ago. But I just realized, your grandmother must live real close by, huh?"

I can't help but stare at his face like I used to, taking in the features I'd been missing for the whatever number of months since he froze me out. God, I've missed looking at him.

My heart thumps faster and faster, the splooshing in my ears getting louder and louder. Not quite what I expected this morning, especially considering this could've been a somewhat pleasurable encounter.

No, seriously, that's three potential encounters, with the three people I can no longer call friends.

Yet I can't help but feel the burden of it all.

Jack speaks again when I don't answer. "So are these for Nana or . . ." And then it dawns on him. "Oh. Has it been a year already?"

I can only nod. Silently. Wordlessly. Very meh-ly.

"Sorry," he says, glancing down at the cash register behind the counter.

A lot is being said in that one word, but I don't know its meaning. This is the first time in months Jack has even glanced my way. I've imagined this interaction so many times, thought about all the things I would say. But now I can't find a single worthy word.

He perks up again, but as if like clockwork, and as if he's used to doing this with other customers. "That'll be fourteen ninety-five."

At this point, all I can do is grab my wallet. Hand over my debit card. And try to keep on moving.

He swipes my card and hands it back. "Hope you have a good day."

29

Yeah, I don't know about that.

My heart pangs with regret. Last year, he'd hardly left my side after Dad died. Now, he's turning back to the flowers and turning his back on me. I know I messed things up with us. I shouldn't have taken advantage of his friendship the way I did. Shouldn't have tried to make it more than it was. In those early days of him icing me out, I was sure he'd get over it and forgive me. But if he can ignore me today of all days, any hope I had wilts with the flowers in this California heat.

I hold on to my delicate purchase and the reserves of whatever strength I have left, and make my departure.

As I walk off, I decide to give him one final look, knowing that it's probably the last time I'm ever going to see him, since I'm never going to step foot anywhere near this damn grocery store again.

God. Why is all this suckage piled on top of me? I'm used to the feeling of missing Dad, knew it would be even worse today, but it's like I've been visited by three ghosts—Holly, Yamany, and Jack—and my heart can barely hold the weight of their haunting.

Back in the car, Nana can only stare at me. As if she's about to say something.

But I can't handle an actual conversation about it.

Especially not about Jack.

As we drive away, my heart plunges all the way to the middle of the Earth, because there he is, spraying at the flowers, sneering away as if full of disgust.

And I can't help but feel like it is directed entirely and a hundred percent toward me.

CHAPTER SEVEN

It'll take us close to an hour to make it to the cemetery even though it's a miracle there's little traffic on the freeway at this time of day.

But it seems like someone next to me can't stop vibrating with nosiness.

"Hazeem, you have to stop," Nana says.

I almost slam on the brakes until it's clear there's no reason to, after scanning all the mirrors. "What do you mean? Do you see an accident up ahead or something?"

Nana twists her gnarled fingers in frustration. "No, no, no, I mean . . . I worry about you. I can't be your best friend. You can't spend all your time with me. You come around almost every day and never seem to want to leave or have anywhere else to go. I love spending time with you, my boy, but you had all these other people you used to hang out with. That Jack boy—you used to see him every day, but at the flower stand, you both barely even looked at each other. What happened?"

My knuckles turn a ghastly pale around the steering wheel. Ugh. I can't have this conversation with her right now. Or ever. Why can't she just accept that I adore spending time with her, especially when she showers me with so much affection. Besides, how do I tell her that it's not exactly my choice to not have any friends besides her? I can't tell her that her grandson is the Leper Loser of LA. "I just love hanging out with you, Nana. And besides, you're not my only friend—you know I also have Mary Shelley."

She shakes her head so hard, she may get a migraine. "Oh God, not that damn rodent again."

"Yes, *my* rodent. And you make it sound like she's a rat."

"Same family, yes? So if the shoe fits . . . in this case, if it looks like a rat, it's a rat. A smaller, rounder kind of rat? Yes. What does she bring you anyway? Apart from potential dysentery or rabies?"

I laugh. "She brings me joy, actually."

"All she does is sleep all day, even the times you've brought her over to my place. That's all she ever does. If I slept as much as she does, I'd be dead."

"Don't say that, Nana."

I want to tell her that I don't mind sleeping all day long. I don't mind lying around in bed, doing nothing. Just staring at the walls, waiting for them to melt. Because it is my summer vacation. I'm supposed to go to college next year. I still have not decided what to do after senior year, but I've got nothing else to look forward to.

Beyond that, how do I explain to her that I've accidentally shrunk my world? See, after my dad died, and when my best friends wanted to have nothing to do with me anymore, I'd decided that I

32

had had enough. I was spent. This machine had run out of gumballs, and there were none left to spit out. Whatever feelings I had left, I decided to wrap them all up into one final figurative gumball, and I left it in the machine somewhere, except maybe it's gotten stuck.

Horrible analogy, and the only thing I can come up with when Nana's right next to me, complaining about . . . me. All I'm saying is that I have very little left to give.

Because "'Tis better to have lost everything but yourself"?

"By the way, I take Mary Shelley for walks in her bubble backpack. And you should see her hamster palace now," I say.

"Good God, Hazeem. Hamster palace. Used to be a hut, then a cottage, then a mansion. How big is it now?"

She's going to hate me so much. "It's almost to the ceiling."

"Hazeem." Her face is frozen in a way that can only be described as if she'd just seen me make out with a pole. "So you're saying it's totally out of control and growing like a wild vine."

"Yeah. But I like taking care of her." Plus, I have nothing else to do. But I don't say that part out loud. "Hey, at least I'm keeping her alive." Which seems to be the weirdest and randomest statement to make.

Nana shakes her head again. "There's something missing in your life. And that is *life*. Which I think you should go get. As in, go 'get a life.'"

"Ha ha. My nana's such a jokester. Old age hasn't failed her yet, and maybe—ouch, why'd you pinch my arm?"

"You like that?" she says. "There's more, I promise. So much strength left in my thumb and forefinger."

Oh, if only she'd realize that it's so much easier for her to tell

33

me to get a life when she's already lived decades of her own. Yeah, so Dad died at thirty-nine. Which only gives me another twenty-two years of living left, if the math of our genes adds up. And is it even worth it, building a life so short?

Maybe there's nothing left to build anything with. Maybe I've given all of it away. Which kinda strikes a gong in me, reverberating all of my insides, seeing how my dad was always the generous one—pretty much "The Giving Tree" personified—and what does he have to show, other than being six feet under?

See, my dad—Mahmoud—was what some would call "free spirited." While my mom would be staring at the ground to make sure she wouldn't trip over anything, he'd be staring at the sky and pointing out a cloud, if he ever saw one in sunny Los Angeles. Then he'd talk about the miracle of a clump of moisture just hovering up there looking like a giant UFO. And if we were at a park, Mom and I would be on our phones, while he'd pull out his sketchbook and doodle and draw, before tearing it out and handing his finished sketch to the first kid he'd see.

One reason why he'd never use an iPad ever. His explanation: art you enjoy is meant to be shared, given away freely, for others to appreciate.

But, of course, he had to make a living, so he still commissioned his masterpieces for hundreds of dollars—sometimes in the thousands if it took weeks to complete. Thank goodness he had some business sense in him.

Anyway. I'm not going to bring any of that up right now. Because I can't bear the thought of summoning up enough energy and resources for twenty-two years of a future I've yet to live. So I'll let my tired grandmother do her complainy bit for as long as she needs to. "Nana, please just be okay with me doing my thing. I'm happy hanging out with you."

"You are not okay," Nana declares as if she knows me better than I know myself. "What about your mother? You really need to try harder with her, you know."

Oh God. I don't even know where to begin with my mom. If every morning is an indicator, it's like trying to move the ocean with a colander—an entirely useless, gargantuan effort. Sometimes, I wonder if she's still human, because, I mean, I don't have to rewind to this morning, or every morning, to remind myself that she's as clockworky and androidy and devoid of emotion as pretty much any other developed AI out there. "Try harder how, Nana?" My voice is louder than I intend. "I've tried my best but she's just too busy for me. Like, she's busy in general, and pretty much drowns herself in it, to the point where even she doesn't feel the need to surface for air. And why am I the one who always has to try? She could try harder, too, you know."

Nana looks off at the mountains ahead of us. "You should have seen her when she first met your dad. I mean, that was if you were even able to. I hardly saw her. He hardly did either, with her in medical school. Your father finally had to make demands on her, that there needed to be a compromise for the relationship to work. They even had a huge argument about it. She said that it was so patriarchal of him to want to stifle her career. And then he explained that a relationship is about two people spending time together, and at that moment in time, the way they were going, they could be single separately and nothing would be any different. That was the most amazing thing about your dad, Hazeem. He could talk sense into anyone. So the compromise was he'd meet her for lunch whenever she was at her university—without holding her or her schedule back—and she'd have to make that one hour free just for him. And she actually did. Her career wasn't affected, she went on to become a resident at an amazing hospital, and they got to see each other one additional brief moment every day."

Sure sounds like my dad.

"I think it was his artistic mind," Nana continues. "It was the way he was able to see the world. I liked watching him paint because every painting he did made me see things in a different light. Remember the one with that kid playing hide-and-seek with that flower? That was just amazing. Like, talk about vision. It still makes me think about how much imagination a child has in their mind."

And then they become a teen like me, and everything around us loses color and turns into a jaded sort of gray.

"You know, I never saw him for who he was until much later in life, and that is my regret. I don't want to make that same mistake with you. So I want you to show me who you really are. Doesn't have to be today. But someday," she says, as she taps on my chest.

I stay quiet for a second, trying to let those words sink in. Do I know who I am? Do I know who I want to be? Because so much of me has been drained away by this past year of barely trying to exist. To say I'm not my previous self is the worst understatement, because I even weigh less. Hmm.

Does a soul have actual weight?

"And you also have to stop shrinking your world, Hazeem," she says.

Whoops. Did she read my mind? "How am I doing that? I don't even know what that means." The lie grows inside me, but maybe she can help point it out, so I can hear it out loud. Since everything is entirely coincidental/accidental/not my fault in the least.

"But that's what you're doing. You've stopped talking to your friends. You've stopped going out. All you do is stay at home. And I don't know how that is healthy for anyone. I'm trying to make you see that."

Here we go again. I feel like we've just talked about this. The funny thing is, sometimes, when I'm just lying around, the world starts to do this blacking out thing. Where I just focus on a flaw on the ceiling, a tiny dot, and everything just disappears, and my vision is filled with just that one speck. And sometimes, the speck grows into this bright ball of particles of nothingness, and, without my doing, starts to take all of me with it.

And then I wake up, and it's hours later. Or the next day.

"I just have to do things my way. Is that okay?" I ask.

"Of course it's okay. I just hope you realize that this world is huge. And that you don't just get your time back. You can choose to explore every corner on this planet and find out what you love about it. Or you can choose to waste it away."

Time's got nothing to do with how I feel. Since I may just be counting down the seconds, days, hours. Hoping for the end? Because I have a feeling there's nothing I can do to fill up any of this time with anything meaningful. I don't care about traveling the world, meeting people, getting my time back.

I just want to waste it all away, letting all of me go. I have no desire to make my world any bigger than it is from outside the

37

confines of my home and Nana's neighborhood. So I think I'll keep going the way I have.

Because who knows what the future will have in store for me. So let it just be me, in Burbank, with Mary Shelley and Nana. Ain't nobody got time for anything else.

CHAPTER EIGHT

We finally drive through the front gates to the Al-Aqsa Cemetery in Pomona with the sun blazing down at us. And even though it's a Monday, the parking lot's half full and there's a smattering of a crowd making its way through the site. I guess everyone's got their special day of visiting.

Seeing all the families gathered makes me wish my mom had joined us. She left just enough hope for me to hold on to, which somehow makes it worse.

And if hope is carried by birds, then there's a ton of it everywhere, with the squawking all over, in the trees. They seem to be really crowing about it.

I grab a pair of folding chairs and umbrellas from the trunk, then carefully extricate my nana out of the passenger seat, letting her grasp my arm like always, as we march through the cars in the parking lot and onto the lushly watered green.

There's something about a burial site that's supposed to summon calm and peace. Yet there's also something else that's obviously eerie about having hundreds of dead people underneath your feet.

Will try not to think about any of the latter.

Nana is quiet as a sudden somberness takes over her. Even her step slows. She knows we're in a hallowed place, and that we must be respectful.

I also wish I'd brought Mary Shelley with me, even if Nana may give her the stinkiest side-eye for being here. But she's always been good, and well-behaved, company.

It takes us a good five minutes of ambling along, as my nana greets the random visitor—some with tears streaming down composed faces—with a warm smile. She knows what pain they must be going through.

The husband who'd lost the wife.

The daughter now without a sister.

And then there's me. The fatherless son.

Finally, after some weaving through on the footpath and following of signs, there he is. Marked by a two-foot granite headstone resembling a minaret, on top of a yellow-tiled grave.

Underneath that sturdy foundation is my father's brittle remains.

Suddenly, my heart aches. A cold seeps through me, trying to leech warmth out of something, anything.

His face pops into my mind, and it's always the same smiley one, even if that mustache would always make him look ridiculously unapproachable and stern. But that's the only one I remember, even as he lay on asphalt down below the Griffith Observatory, exhaling his last breaths . . . and once more, his final words that never made sense to me pop back into my mind.

"Count not the years."

Then his hand went limp and crashed onto my lap. But still, he left this world with a shadow of a smile. Almost as if he knew he left only good behind.

Good memories? Maybe. A good me? Highly debatable, seeing how I'm nowhere near whatever the definition of "good" may be.

Nana lets go of me and offers a silent prayer to my dad, and all I can do is breathe deep, while leaning one hand and my entire body weight against the folding chairs resting on the firm grass.

Am I going to be fine? Am I going to make it through this?

I wish I could convince myself that I never will—or can—be fine. Because everyone operates on some level of dysfunction that will never let them get to the far-right of that meter. Especially for someone who's at the start of his second year of asking, "Okay, what now?"

So all I can do is focus my energy on something small. Something achievable. Before my whole world tears itself apart at the seams. And the task I decide to tackle is to pull apart the folding chairs and set them down, since my poor nana needs something to rest on.

She's already eyeing them with a raised eyebrow.

Three seconds later, I award myself five thousand points for a job well done. "There you go, Nana. I know you've been waiting."

She slaps my forearm. "Don't be cheeky, Hazeem. Your nana's

bones are weary. They've got nowhere to go but down. Like this."
She plants herself in one of the chairs, then pulls out her tiny Koran,
flips the pages, and starts muttering a sura to herself.

I pop the umbrellas open, to provide her with shade on this
sunny day.

Welp. Here we are. She's going to be at it for a while.

I stay for a few of the suras, saying the requisite responses, but
after a while it all starts to weigh on me. An entire year—31,536,000
heartbeats—without Dad. Despite the fresh outdoor air, my breathing feels stifled.

"I'm going to take a quick stroll. Check out the lay of the land,"
I say, getting up to leave. Just feeling a little fidgety, since we're
going to be here practically all day anyway.

She watches me skulk away, then focuses back on the headstone. Soon the tears will start pouring, until there's no more.

I don't remember the last time I did that. Not for the entire year.
I know I cried when Dad died, but after that, my tear ducts closed
up shop.

Which Nana thinks is super weird.

Yet I can't bring myself to do it. Tried many times. Nothing
would ever appear out of my eyes. The well had dried up, never to
be filled again.

Maybe I'm still in shock. Maybe I'm just mad at him. Maybe
I'll get over it one day and I'll cry an entire ocean. But that won't
be today.

I'm not feeling it anyway. I'm just numb.

I suddenly find myself having wandered off to a far corner of
the cemetery, and there are only two other families within view—
a young couple and an elderly woman with two middle-aged

men—but I make sure to keep an eye on Nana, and keep a tight radius, as I explore the grounds.

Everyone's intensely praying for their loved ones. I hope the people they are mourning weren't taken too soon like my dad. Except, on closer inspection, the young couple stares down at a burial plot half the size of my dad's. And then the truth strikes me. God, what a loss they've had to endure. How old was their child? I've overheard my mom and Nana discuss how unfortunate it is for a parent to lose their child. The pain is unimaginable and incomparable, like suddenly losing the sun one day and not knowing what warmth can ever feel like again.

Though I can't help feeling a little selfish about my own circumstances. Because sometimes I wonder what it would be like if I had gone first. Not having to worry about if my mom goes. Not feeling this pain that never seems to go away. Because I still haven't gotten over losing my dad. It's a pain I can never understand. A pain that still to this day feels like a black hole in my chest that wants to swallow every ray of light.

The hot summer sun beats down on me. Sweat drips down my back.

As I continue my walk, with so many of the dead around me, I find it hard to be close to my dad's grave, so I continue to stray around the outskirts, alongside the wall that separates us from the outside world.

I just wish I had been given the chance to spend the rest of my life with him. It's almost as if I've been cheated. Everything that I should have had with him taken away.

For the second time today, I wish I could travel back to the past, to also warn him about that day.

If only there was a way.

Because, seriously. What I would give to have another year with him. I'd trade everything in this world just for that chance. I would tear this whole universe apart, star after star. Everything in it fed to the black hole monster I'll become, just so I can spend one more day with him.

Except I'm not a monster. Maybe just grumpy. Am I hungry? No, I had a cookie on the drive earlier. That's the weird thing about grief: it can make it impossible to know what you want or need.

I continue to march the perimeter of the cemetery, until, for some odd reason, when I glance back at Nana, she seems to be still.

No longer in prayer.

And with her chin glued to her chest.

CHAPTER NINE

She's just sitting there. Arms hanging limp. Head leaning to one side. Koran in her lap.

Nana's a strong woman. She's always said that. Made certain of it.

Yet as I hurry my way back to my dad's plot, it's very obvious something is wrong.

Because she's more still than a dead person.

My entire stomach suddenly fills with oily panic. My fingers race to her wrist, to check for a pulse, my phone in the other hand on the ready to punch those three important digits.

And just like that, the sudden realization dawns on me.

There's no pulse. And I'm about to lose her.

I only have precious moments.

As luck would *not* have it, all the families nearby have left. And

I don't know what to do, except for the one thing that I know has worked.

Although, will it work again? It has on everyone else. I've got to try.

I'm about to say the words when someone appears in my periphery.

At first glance, it looks like a woman. She's got a pixie cut, and she's in neon-orange overalls, as if she's just escaped from prison. Or she's been sentenced to picking up trash by the freeway. I can't really tell.

At another glance, my eyes obviously must be deceiving me, because she looks like Sandra Bullock. Yes, *that* Sandra Bullock— that actress my dad adored—which can't be, because this is a cemetery. And I don't know what she's doing here unless she's in the area filming a prison break movie? And she's decided to wander off?

Should I ask her for help?

No, I can handle it. I know what to do.

I just have to do this once again.

Figure out that it can work.

And I'm about to say the words when this Sandra Bullock wannabe, but a younger version definitely closer to my age, suddenly appears next to me.

Her face full of warning, she utters the words, "Do not do it."

I'm taken aback. "Huh? What do you mean? How'd you get here so fast? And who are you, lady?"

She balks, a finger wagging in my face. "Lady? Excuse us. We do not look like a . . . Whatever, never mind. Do not say the words, Hazeem."

Eh? "How do you know my name?"

She's mere inches from me. "If you do it, you will be in big trouble. We *all* will be in big trouble."

"I don't know who you are, but I need to help my grandmother. We can talk after." So I say the words: "Twenty-two years. For my nana."

Then suddenly, everything goes quiet.

The lady can only shake her head, while being very close to yanking out fistfuls of her hair. "We told you. We told you not to do it. But would you listen to us? Of course you wouldn't listen to a stranger, especially someone who's well aware of the consequences for what you were about to do. Anyway, you're in big trouble now, do you hear us? Why do you look like you've just swallowed an entire planet? Can you hear us? Nod three times if you can."

I have no idea what she's saying, but the one thing I know is that something is dreadfully wrong.

Because the birds have stopped squawking.

CHAPTER TEN

But I don't have a second to think much of it, since my feet stomping on the grass is pretty loud right now. In fact, it's the only thing to even make a sound.

Other than the pumping of my heart drumming in my ears.

Yes, I'm trying to run away from the young Sandra Bullock lookalike. Seriously, what is she doing here, of all places, and did she have super amazing Botox or surgery or whatever, because I've seen the movies my dad would force my mom to watch, that she'd roll her eyes at, and this young lady in orange looks a hundred thousand percent just like she does, but decades younger.

And I'm also running because I need to get help.

While dialing 911, but getting nowhere, because . . . all that's coming through is dead air.

Fast walking now. Because my heart and nerves can't take this much excitement. While glancing back again and again.

But she just stands there, next to Nana, staring at me. So bright in those neon-orange overalls. Head cocking left and right. Almost as if she's waiting for . . . something. But definitely not me, because I'm busy trying to get help.

She rolls her eyes and waves at me to come back, but that's not happening.

There's got to be security in this place.

I keep dialing and speed-walking. Maybe if I can get to the parking lot, someone will let me—

Damn, I know this place is not quite a maze, but it sure takes me a few minutes to find my bearings.

I keep working my way forward, glancing back at the disappearing figure of is-she-really-Sandra Bullock, then up at the sky for no reason, then all around me.

And that's when I see a couple just standing there, on the walkway. Oh, it's the husband and wife who'd lost a child.

My heart plunges to my stomach at seeing their backs, his arm around her waist, because I have zero intention of disrupting their moment.

But I have to.

So I make my way to them. Hoping they can help me. And when I'm a few steps behind, I say out loud to announce my presence, "Excuse me, sir. Miss, could I borrow your phone? Mine's having a problem, and I can't seem to get connected."

Nothing.

They're literally statues. Unmoving. And it seems they can't hear a word I'm saying.

Which I think is kind of rude. I'm clearly desperate! Okay, fine, maybe they're going through so much grief right now that their eardrums continue to ring with their constant sobbing, but Nana isn't going to make it if I can't find a working phone.

I run past them and plant myself in front of their faces. This fool with the panicky face. "Excuse me, please. I'm sorry to interrupt, but is it possible for me to use your phone and—"

Odder and odder.

Their faces are contorted as if they're in the middle of sharing a story. Up close, it's obvious they've shed a few tears. Their brown cheeks—as brown as mine—have visible glimmery tracks on them, and their eyes are red-rimmed.

They're . . . frozen.

And as I stand here, my heart thumping louder and louder, it's suddenly eclipsed by the silence that's as bright as a full moon. It thunders, creating a ringing in my ears.

There's just absolute nothing.

Nothing but quiet.

How is this possible?

I take in everything around me—the trees and their branches and leaves—and the realization hits me hard.

Nothing is moving. There's no rustling. Not even the distant whooshing of cars. Just deathly quiet.

Which makes me spin three hundred and sixty degrees, again and again, getting more and more confused, while getting dizzier and dizzier.

What in the hell is going on?

Am I trapped in the afterworld of an afterlife? Is everyone dead and I'm stuck all alone, destined to keep walking this earth without knowing the reason why this happened?

I have to ground myself, otherwise all my thoughts will escape into the atmosphere, leaving me thoughtless.

So I think about the one person who'd been good about calming me down—my dad.

Once, a long time ago, he told me that life is all about losing yourself, so you can find yourself. Which took me a while to understand.

Am I lost now? But what am I searching for?

I settle on the man and woman in front of me for answers. What were they trying to say to each other? Were they exchanging pacifying words, to reassure themselves that their lives can and should go on, even after such a devastating loss?

My mind settles on Sandy B. Did she do this?

Except that this . . . *all this* . . . is beyond the comprehension of my tiny lizard brain. And that brain is telling me flight's the only solution.

So I dash my way to the parking lot, stumbling along while trying to hold on tight to a reality that's quickly slipping away. Because everything is frozen.

No one and nothing is moving except for me.

It looks like a very well-coordinated prank. But, like, specifically for me.

"Do you understand what we're trying to tell you now," says the same voice from five minutes ago.

I spin on my heels and there she is, as garishly bright as ever in those criminal overalls. "Who are you?"

She simply folds her arms and shifts her weight to one side, while casting the judgiest look ever. "Who are we? Are you really asking us who we are, little Hazeem? Now is not the time for explanations. So, listen to us. You are in the worst kind of trouble. Like a yachtload in a sewerage, if we have to properly compare it to. And we mean every sense of the word. Deep, gigantic, sinking, stinking trouble. Nope, we can't even *guess* how we're about to fix this, but we're open to suggestions."

"Fix what? What did I do? And why are you calling yourself 'we'?"

"We should not have to explain ourself. Because you've just been caught committing the most heinous crime of crimes."

My heart's about to explode from all this action and confusion. "Crime? What crime?"

"A timecrime."

I just stare at her.

She stares back. "You've never heard of a timecrime, have you?"

"Uh, no. Listen, this is all just a big misunderstanding. I didn't mean to take this timecrime thing—"

"A timecrime *is* the crime; it's not a thing that's— Never mind. Let's not bother with that. You should very well know the very thing you've taken from us."

"But I *don't!*" My exasperation only grows with everything that comes out of this lady's mouth. "Will you please just tell me what it is so I can try to find it and return it to you?"

"That's just it. You can't just put time back."

My heart must've positively stopped, because I don't think I heard that right. "I'm sorry. What? Wait, who are you?"

"Isn't it obvious?" She gives the most exaggerated flourish of a hand, then says, "We are the one. The only. Time."

CHAPTER ELEVEN

If this is a joke, someone needs to tickle me or something, because there are no giggles to be had. "Say that again? You're . . ."

She gives a bow, then a curtsy, then air kisses. "Time. Like . . . *the* Time."

"*The* Time? Like you're a minute? A second? An hour? A clock? An Apple Watch?"

She rolls her eyes. "We're all of it. We are Time. Time is us. You know Fate? Luck? Death? Yes, by that very odd nod you've got going on, and those eyes as large as doubloons, you obviously know who they are, so then think along the same line, but . . . Time." Followed by a splaying of her hands, as if to say "Ta-da!"

I must look as plopped out as I feel. Just absolutely smacked around.

So she continues on. "Look, we'll show you something quite impressive."

Another flourish of her hands, and with a snap of her fingers . . .

A glittering golden sphere pops into view, hovering next to her shoulder. She leans against it as if it can bear all her weight. Then she grabs it and tosses it around as if to juggle it, but gives up since she can't really do that with one ball. Then she lobs it over to me.

I swat it away clumsily with an unflattering grunt, and it drifts right back to its owner. "I don't want whatever that thing is!"

"You're going to hurt its feelings," she says, her face an odd combination of crestfallen and disgust.

"It has emotions?"

This just keeps getting weirder and weirder.

Her face uncontorts itself, and she pastes on a sickly, maniacal, wide-mouthed smile that looks totally unnatural. "No, it does not. But we're not here to explain our Chronosphere to you, because you did something bad. And you need to fix it."

"You keep saying that, but I did not steal any time. How does anyone steal time anyway?" I ask, my curiosity getting the better of me. I shouldn't even be entertaining this conversation, but maybe if I go along with it enough, this elaborate prank will finally end.

"You just disrupted the timeline . . . timeline . . . timeline . . ."

Why is there an echo and where is it coming from? "You have no clue how to explain things so anyone can actually understand them, do you?"

She slaps her forehead. "Fine. Let us explain it in the most humansensical way we can think of. You owe us, the ever glorious

54

and generous Time, a debt. A time debt. Because you are running in the deficit."

"But you just said I stole time—now it's a debt? And you still haven't told me how you know my name."

"We know a lot of things, okay! Like, a *lot* lot. A very big amount of a lot. The lottest of lots there ever will be. Because we're Time." She ends that with another curtsy, that orange jumpsuit looking quite out of place with the action.

"Just because you keep saying you're Time doesn't make it make any more sense. You're not . . . God, are you?"

"How many times do we have to tell you? We're *Time*. This is, like, the seventy-third time we're saying that. How many more times do we have to say it? We swear, by the time our time together has ended, we'd have said 'time' eleventy-three hundred and nine times more," she says, with a wrinkle of her nose.

"Okay, stop saying 'time' already."

Honestly, even as she's throwing a tantrum, she looks pretty moviestar-ish, with that slicked-back hair and that very unique nose. Up close, she's got the most natural makeup on, too. As if it's all effortless.

"Fine, you're Time," I say, very much to a shake of my head, because this is just a little too hard to believe.

"You just said it," she says.

Very much to a glare from me.

Which earns a grin from her. "Now that we've established who we are, let's just say we're in charge of everything chronological."

"Like, all of time?"

Time slaps her hands on her thighs, then points to the ground. "Look here. Down here."

I can only narrow my eyes as I focus on what she's looking at.

A second later, something sprouts out, like the tail of an animal, until it juts even farther out, growing an inch. Then another. Then seconds later, a foot of something green, which turns into something brown. A minute passes, and it's an actual plant.

Another minute, and it's a young tree twice as tall as I am, with actual branches.

"There you go," Time says. "See, when we're in this state, time moves in different ways. Manipulating time molecules that only we are capable of interacting with. Everything outside our radius is suspended in time."

I stare at the tree, reaching a hand toward it to make sure it's real. When I touch rough bark, that's when I know: all of this—the frozen world, this ridiculous Time person, the gold glowing orb with feelings—is real.

"So you're saying," and I can't help the gulp and the sudden sweats, "that the world stopping in its tracks, it's all happening because of . . . me?"

CHAPTER TWELVE

She scoffs, with a hand on her chest. "You are finally catching on. Took you nearly a millennium with that one, didn't it? Yes. It's all your doing. And we, Time, are here to make sure everything is righted back to its right way," she says, as she points toward her golden sphere.

"We? You and . . ." I say, pointing to the floaty thing.

"We, as in yes. Us and this thing here. Together. We calculate everything there is to do with a timeline or timelines."

"Wait a sec. So are *you* Time, or are you two *together* Time?"

"Don't bother trying to fold that into your noggin nuggets and just play along. For now, you may refer to us as 'us,' or we as 'the both of you.' Like, 'gosh, don't they look amazing with that glittery golden ball floating next to them?'"

"Oh okay, thanks for clearing that up. You go by 'they'—got it.

But what exactly is it . . . this ball of yours that you so casually toss around?"

"The Chronosphere?" ~~she says~~ they say, a little hesitant. "Think of it as a documentation device."

"Documentation? As in, it's recording everything right now?"

"Yes, it's recording everything everywhere everywhen all at once." They wave away any further attempt at an explanation. "Hazeem, we're about to break some bad news to you. What you've been doing—wishing for whatever or whomever to be saved—you've been doing it all wrong."

Okay, this is my time to shine, and maybe confuse them, too. "I know for a fact that they're not just wishes. See, I've got a super-power." That's something I've never told anyone. It even sounds a little silly coming out of my mouth—but it's true. It's how Mary Shelley has lived as long as she has. It's how Holly survived her accident—and even if they don't know it, it's why she, Yamany, and Jack no longer speak to me. "But how do you know?"

"We told you we know—"

"Everything, yes. But all I've been doing is asking for people to . . . rejoin the living. Those who've really needed it. And it's worked! I've made that happen."

I don't know how or why, but I've been able to save the people I love—or, loved—from leaving me like Dad did. Although I guess it'd be more accurate to say I prevented them from dying. Because in the end, with the exception of Mary Shelley, they all still left me. But that wasn't going to stop me from trying the same thing with my nana, too.

Time tut-tut-tuts. "No, you haven't, Hazeem. You think you have. But, no. In truth, you've been doing something truly grave.

They were supposed to die. Their time was up. Where do you think the extensions of their lives came from?"

"From . . . why does it have to come from somewhere? I helped the people and creature I care about most. How can that be criminal?"

Time grasps their chin, as if suddenly sagacious. "Our dear boyling. Every single time you've wished for someone to be saved— including your delightfully frozen hamster—it means years are taken away from . . . somewhere. In this case, a specific someone. Care to venture a guess . . . who . . . from?" they say, suddenly wiggling their eyebrows.

What.

No.

Can't be.

The truth tsunamis its way to me, threatening to rip apart the already teetering foundation every part of me is hanging onto. "You're saying it's not a superpower?"

Their look turns even more grim, with no humor to it. "Only humanchilds believe in superpowers. You are a near-adult. The nonsensical should have been evicted from your sinewy cerebellum years ago."

"Oh my God. Do you think this is funny?"

"We do not do funny. We don't even do fun. We don't know anything about the emotions that plague your kind. Right, Chronosphere?"

The metallic ball seems to nod, if that's at all possible.

But they continue. "Everything has a balance in the ledger of this universe. And you cannot just give away life without taking it from somewhere. And in your case . . . We had to make our appearance known—something we're not a huge fan of—when you were about to grant your grand-nana additional life, which is a grand-nono. But you did it anyway, you stubborn fool of a person-thing. And now, your lifeline is in the deficit."

I am truly speechless.

They wave a hand at me. "Yes, speechless, are you? That's right. You've given away more years than you had left, putting yourself and the entire timeline you live in in danger. The life you have left is in the negative. As in, less than zero. Do you understand every-thing now?"

CHAPTER THIRTEEN

I've been giving my own years away?" I can't help but shake my head at this realization. "But I had to. I had to bring my nana back to life again. I can't let her go."

"Exactprecisely. All of this is unprecedentsia. Very new stuff," Time says, with a crack of their knuckles.

So close to slamming my palms to my ears. "I don't want to hear this. Please, just stop."

Maybe if I close my eyes, too, they'll disappear?

Gone are all my internal organs. Seems like every vital piece has been ground up, puréed into mush. Yes, my inside is a hundred percent slurry at this point.

I remember wishing for a very specific superpower, way back when Dad had introduced me to the Marvel Cinematic Universe. Forget flying or invisibility or super-cosmic-human strength.

I wanted to be able to stop time. It was the most fundamental power that would let me achieve anything I wanted.

Late for school? Well, *almost* late, since I can stop time in the one second before the bell rings and casually crawl my way over through the front gates.

Want to build muscles to get out of this scrawny body? Pause! And I can take whatever time I need to go to the gym and work out for months and all that. Bet it's not hard to turn this lime-size bicep into a cantaloupe.

Now, I just want to . . . stop Time. From trying to convince me all of this is real.

But here they are, standing next to me. In their bright orange-ness. "So what do I have to do?"

"We're thinking . . . we've got to reverse what you did. As in, retrieve some of your time back."

"What? That's it?" I expected the solution to be far more complicated, considering how confusing this whole interaction has been.

"Of course. What else did you expect?" Time says, with a folding of their arms across their chest. "Does your person expect something grander, fanfare of some sort? Shall you need fireworks?"

"Okay, so just to get things straight once more, all I have to do is take back the time I've given to others and return it to my time-line. Is that right?"

Time regards me with a cocked head. "We've gone through this. And we shall go through it one more time for your reluctant skull flesh to comprehend. We just have to take back the deficit. And voilà, you're done."

Ah. Should I even ask what I actually owe? Because if I do, then I guess I'll know to what age I'll live? Because apparently, having granted four beings life, I'm supposed to live to nearly a hundred?

Ha! Why would I want to live that long? I mean, why would anyone want to? Because I'll outlive everyone, while I get to watch the younger generations prance around like they own the damn world.

I give Nana a glance. She goes through life pretty much invisible to everyone around her, and I think the one reason she secretly enjoys having me around all the time is because I do see her. All of her.

Okay. Anyway.

Time's explanation is pretty straightforward, though something else nags at me. "Is there any other way? You're Time. Can't you just fix it on your own?"

Time grits their teeth. "If we could, we would've. Thought we'd give you an explanation. A do-over. A chance to choose."

The sweats are starting again, streaming out of every pore. "What? Choose what?"

And then the nagging continues. And I'm pretty sure I'm close to grasping what it is. I think they want me to—

"Shall we get started?" Time says, as they swish around in their orange overalls.

And with a snap of their fingers . . .

✦ ✦ ✦

"How did we get back to my house?"

We've gone from the searing brightness of the green that was the cemetery, to the bland whiteness of my "living" room.

Time merely offers a casual glance at everything around us. "See, that is one aspect of the specialness of being us. We can do something like traverse time and space and bring us to wherever we want to be," Time says as they march back and forth. "Your living arrangements look . . . What's the proper word? Spartan? We would like to say definitely roomy. Is that thing what you human-peoples call a couch? Oh, and we think hidden in that blocky thing made out of tree," they say, pointing to the credenza, "is what you would call a television? You play moving pictures with loud sounds from it, we've heard?" They pat it like it's a good boy. "There you are. But we have one very good reason to be here," Time says, as they put a spring in their step all the way to the window, where the bubble dome backpack still sits, unmoved.

God, I wonder if Mary Shelley's all right, as I rush over and notice she's frozen, too. Just like everything else we've come across.

Which sucks so bad, as dryness leeches all moisture from my throat. This is all because of me. "Can you unfreeze her, please? She shouldn't be a victim of my timecrime."

Time shrugs, scratches their chin at what looks to be a very important decision. "We surmise that's doable, seeing how she is the subject of our very important discussion."

And with a flick of their wrist . . .

Mary Shelley is instantly unfrozen, her beady eyes staring at both of us from the bubble dome. *Eh, what's going on, and who's this weirdo?*

"Watch your furry little unwashed mouth," Time says. "Because flattery will most certainly get you everywhen."

Huh. "You can hear her?" I ask.

Time nods. "And she surely is a loudmouth, for such a tiny little thing. Bet she gets pythons excited, doesn't she? Oh, don't give me that look, boyperson. Snakes gotta live somehow."

"Don't be wicked to Mary Shelley," I say, as I grab a baby carrot stick from the backpack's side compartment and hand it to her through the feeding hole.

She grabs it and starts munching on it. Eyes almost full of knowledge.

Thank goodness she's fine.

"Okay, so how do I do this?" I ask.

"Don't you understand? The answer is right here," Time says with a pointy finger.

I stare at Mary Shelley and then at Time and then back at Mary Shelley, and then out the window. And then back at Mary Shelley. "You're not suggesting what I think you're suggesting."

"What do you suggest that I'm suggesting that you're suggesting that I'm suggesting?"

My head's starting to pound. "That I take time away from Mary Shelley."

Yup. That nagging feeling is back.

"Well, thank you for suggesting that. She's definitely an interesting subject. Since she's obviously the easiest option, isn't she? We think we should just go ahead. Let's do it, so our story can conclude; we say 'The End' to our current conundrum, and we can go back to doing what we have to—making sure all of time runs smoothly and without any more hitches."

I need them to spell it all out. "Wait—what happens when we take time back from her?"

"Well, her timeline will end of this very moment. And whatever is left will be returned to you. Which shall fix it all."

"But that would mean . . ." The realization that had already hit me is now being etched out very clearly. "You want me to kill my hamster?"

"We were hoping you wouldn't figure that out."

My heart skips several beats at potentially losing my most favorite pet. "You can't just take away a life like that. She means something to me. More than something. Almost everything!"

"*You* are the one who took away life, Hazeem. The timeline is in trouble because of you, and you need to fix it."

I grab the backpack and clutch Mary Shelley closer.

How do I explain to Time that she has weathered the past lonesome year with me? That if it hadn't been for her, I don't think I could have made it. She is my therapy animal, my comfort animal, my soul animal, whatever anyone wants to call her. She has helped me more than anyone or anything else has. She's my security blanket. All of the above rolled up into one. Without her, I would've felt completely alone. "Is there no other option? There has to be something else."

"This is the easiest. This hamster is worth very little in the grand scheme of things." Time says as they seem to weigh Mary Shelley with a squinty eye, measuring her with both hands.

"How can you say that? Just because she's one-hundredth my size doesn't mean she's not worthy of being carefully weighted against anything else."

"Let's see . . . The average lifespan of a rodent such as itself is two years," Time says with a flutter of their lashes and a crossing of the arms and a tapping of their foot on the floor as if impatiently waiting a decision. "That's one-fortieth of the maximum human lifespan. Maximum-ish. We know your kind can grow a bit older. But also, this tiny little thing that cannot talk and can only eat and poop out little pellets, based on what we've noticed, will never be worth as much as your life."

I don't know if my life is worth anything. That's one thing I'm trying to grapple with at this moment. At least Mary Shelley brings me joy, even with her diminutive size. But what is my purpose? What do I bring to everyone's table? To an outsider watching, I seem like nothing more than a burden.

"Why are your eyebrows all knotted like that?" Time asks. "Why do you look worried and full of rumination? We thinks a bit of lightening up will help. Do you want to do some juggling?"

They pull out the Chronosphere from one pocket and wink at me.

It's meant to be a distraction, but I won't let this go. "You don't understand. Every living thing that has a life is equal to each other."

"What about the chicken or cows that your kind love to consume? That's ending their lives before they're allowed to live to the fullest, isn't it?"

Welp. That's got me stumped. "Like you said, we . . . *gotta live somehow.*"

"That's kind of a double standard, isn't it?" Time says. "The fact that you humanspecimens seem to value life equally and then suddenly do a double take when it comes to eating an animal off a plate. So, what is it?"

"What do you mean?"

"What do we do with the hamster?"

Mary Shelley chitters in my hands, as if she understands the negotiation and is begging for her life.

Don't worry, Mary Shelley, I tell her telepathically. *I won't let anything happen to you.*

I turn back to Time. "Look, I'd like to know all my options before making up my mind. Mary Shelley isn't the only being I've given life to, right?"

I don't tell them that I'm thinking there's got to be a loophole of some sort, an escape hatch to help me get out of this conundrum. "Does the timeline have some kind of . . . deadline?"

Time bounces the Chronosphere from one hand to the other, as if bored. "No, technically we're frozen. We can be frozen for all of eternity. The timeline doesn't have to move. But that's just it— the timeline will not go back to its previous state until you decide what to do. Because if we unfreeze it, everything will blow up into nothingness. And we don't want that. Do we?"

An intrusive thought pops into my brain: Would that be so bad? I mean, I'm not having the best time ever. I don't know if Time is helping me any more than I want to be helped. Still, I wipe the thought away.

Time shakes their head. "We can see you're thinking hard, but we think the value of our words haven't lent their full severity. When we say the timeline is frozen for all eternity, we do mean it. This is basically the end of existence as you know it. The price of your carelessness."

"Wait, what. The end . . . of everything?"

"Precisecompletely. Think about it. If the timeline doesn't

move, then nothing exists anymore. Does it? Not in the real sense of the word. If one doesn't move forward in time, one is simply present and never a part of the future. So yes, the future ceases to exist, and hence, existence ends."

Time says those words with no expression on their face. It's just a smooth mask. As if they are indifferent to it as well, even if their words so far suggest the total opposite.

But.

Oh. My. God. That's the largest pill I have to swallow ever. That is a major universe-shattering deal right there. It's like one of those popular tales of someone being the key to the destruction or salvation of their planet, and no matter what, they end up doing the right thing—because they had to. Because it was expected of them. Because they had no choice?

The only difference in this case is . . . me.

And do I even care?

But do I even care?

Well . . . do I even care?

I mean, yes, I should, because this whole existence is not just about me. It's about eight billion people and countless others spread throughout the entire universe, and in future unborn worlds, and all the potential that it contains.

But I'm no martyr. I don't want to be. Look what asking for others to be saved, and accidentally gifting the years of my life, has wrought upon us cowing heathens?

Ugh. I've got to stop with the Shakespearean dramatics.

Seriously though, am I not allowed to be selfish for just one microsecond to figure out what I can and should do? So, the world

I know is over, entirely gone, in a poof, until I make a decision. And if I make the wrong decision, then I'll be flambéing the entire universe.

But until then: "Once again, I'm begging you to just let me go through all of my options? Please?"

Time blinks once. Twice. "You're saying you don't care that everything we have known so far is indeed . . . *dun dun dun?* Hmm. Peculiar how you humanlings handle things during times of crises."

"It's not that I don't care. It's just that, if we are totally done, then can I have a moment to figure out how best to . . . *undone* everything?"

"Suits you. We guess everyone's existence shall gladly depend on your mindmaking." Time rolls their eyes, slaps their face, and yawns out loud. "Fine. We'll do it your way for a bit. But just a little bit. Like a thousandth of a microsecond."

There's something inherently odd about them—besides the whole mythical being thing. "Why is it everything you do is so exaggerated? It's like watching a very bad B-movie."

"What do you mean?" they say, with a widening of their eyes and a loud gasp.

"The crossing the arms, the tapping the toe? It's like you're also a very bad actor."

Time shakes their head. "Well, forgive us for trying. We've opted to make you more comfortable with us by appearing human . . . ish. We heard orange is a very human color. Greatly complements skins of all types? And we thinks this face is familiar to you?"

I'm stumped by their assumptions. But I finally find my words. "Can you just . . . be yourself?"

"But we are ourself. We don't have a self. We are Time. Don't you understand? Okay, we're done. Moving on to the next victim."

"What do you—"

Time puts on a grin. "Relax, childlet. We're doing it your way, remember? When we snap our fingers, everything will be— wait. Why do you have that face? That looks like you're planning something very unexpected."

CHAPTER FOURTEEN

Maybe there is something wrong with me. "What if I don't want to? I mean, maybe I'm facing a sudden mini existential crisis, but what's the point of all this? Of everything? Of repairing the timeline, even?"

Time twists their facial parts into an odd expression. "Do you see this face we're making? We think this is what you call rage. And it's caused by your sudden indecision on saving the universe, thus spelling its doom. Do you want us to make an even ragier face?"

Oh God. How do I explain to them that there's no way I can get angry at that face? Seeing how the eyes are so bulbous like that and the nose is all scrunched up and the teeth fully gritted—they look just like an anglerfish.

And so, I laugh.

No. Seriously. I actually laugh. Not a giggle, but an actual throaty laugh that bursts from my lungs. A strange sound I haven't heard in a while. A long time, even. Feels weird, like my body's not used to it, and must now adjust to how it makes me feel. But a shudder overcomes it all, and I turn back to the cause of my strange predicament. "You need to do a better job of figuring out what facial expressions are supposed to look like."

But—and it's a big one!—I did just laugh, didn't I?

Time wags a finger in my face as they tower over me. "What are you thinking now? It looks like you're ready to consume a heavy dose of emotional fiber, to facilitate with emotional digestion?"

"Oh, don't be mean. Wait, can you read my thoughts?"

"We cannot. We may only reflect upon what we see with our very own eyes. And you're no longer allowed to hmm and oh-no and huh your way through this. All right, enough then. You're coming with us."

Time points to Mary Shelley and me, snaps their fingers, and poof . . .

✦ ✦ ✦

We're back at the cemetery, twenty feet from Nana. Me plus the bubble dome backpack on my chest.

"Here we go. It's just us again," Time says with a flourish of their hands.

Ugggghhhhhh. "What are we doing back here?"

Mary Shelley looks equally dazed. *No, seriously, what is happening?*

"Well, since you refused to revisit your former victims, or take away the life from something very easily decided on—yes, we're looking directly at that bubble on your chesticle—we shall have to move forward. We think it's very obvious what we have to do," Time says.

They point a finger at Nana.

"Excuse me? Do you actually have the nerve to suggest what I think you're suggesting?" I can't even allow myself to be speechless at the suggestion because what in the actual flying—

But Time's face is very matter-of-fact. "Let her go. You have got to let her go."

How do I explain to them that I've dumped almost everything in my life? Not just people, but almost every possession that I own, including my own brain. Sometimes I wonder if my hypothalamus and amygdala and cerebral cortex and hippocampus are all just waiting around, shrugging and side-eyeing each other for something to *feel* about because . . . yeah, there's not much going on.

Because there's just too much space.

But they all know my nana's untouchable. It's my turn to wag a finger in Time's face. "I am not going to let my nana go. She's the only person who understands everything about me. I know she's also seventy-five and she likely won't live much longer, but I need her to stay around to take care of me."

Time starts to make their way to Nana. "We don't think you realize how above the average lifespan of your kind she's had. It's not very typical for someone to live over seventy-three point two, you know. Wait, you do know this, don't you?"

"My dad only lived to thirty-nine, so . . . You know what, I'm hopping off this train of thought onto another, because suddenly I'm wondering why Nana had my dad later in life—like at thirty-five? There's still so much for me to find out from her." I have to make

Time understand what will be lost if I let Nana go. That all the time I take back from her won't be worth the time I'll lose with her.

Time scrunches up their face, then pulls out the Chronosphere from their back pocket and confers with it in a hushed voice. Then they tuck it away. "Well, if you think about it . . . as in, if you let her go, then you can let your dad go."

I'm stunned at the suggestion. That's what everyone tells you to do after someone dies—let it go, let them go.

My dad's smile comes to mind again. The way he used to look at me even when I did the most ridiculous thing, like spill milky cereal out of my mouth because I was gulping it down too damn fast while playing a game. All I'd hear was the chuckle, and I'd pause the game and find him staring with wide eyes at me—which I think could've been wonder?—but I'd just scoff and tell him he was making me uncomfortable.

Then he'd run over behind the couch and kiss me on the head, before disappearing into his study.

Most of the time, I'd just ignore it, but there was a moment or two when I'd keep the game paused, and just sit there, basking in my dad's affection.

What I would give to just be near him once again, let alone have him smile at me.

But I shake my head. "My dad was the most important person to me next to Nana and Mary Shelley. You're suggesting I let go of that. You do know this, right?"

Time merely chews at a thought before leveling a gaze so intense, it's hard not to do a double take at it. "We don't. We don't know anything of the emotional relationship between humankinds. We are mainly interested in keeping the timeline correct and on the right path, which you seem very interested in sabotaging. So, we shall ask you a pertinent question: Are you going to be friend or foe? Are you going to let this universe continue on its path of frozen destruction, or revive it and let us continue with our work? Because as you very well know, we don't have to give you a choice."

So . . . is Time my enemy? Or my friend?

Glurg. That's the sound my throat's making. "I'm not your enemy. No one is. Just . . . just don't make me let her go."

"You do realize your nana will eventually die?" A pause. "Every one of you will? We have heard that it's a curse all of you peoplebeings are inflicted with."

Oh, if only I'm allowed to smack someone without any consequences. "Well, I want to hold on to her for as long as I can stay alive."

Time stares at Nana, then at me. "But you don't know when *you* will die."

But the thing is, I do. Not really, I guess, but for the past year I've felt deep down that Dad and I would meet the same fate.

So I say out loud what I never have before. "I figured I was going to die around the same time as my dad. That I wouldn't make it past his age, thirty-nine. See, he was healthy. He was fit. There's no reason he should have had a heart attack, let alone a fatal one. Now, look at me. I'm in this undernourished, alfalfa sprout body. I don't even work out and I don't do anything healthy to keep my heart working."

Time merely shrugs. "We think there are many decisions you have to make, but it looks like we're not going anywhere without you deciding. Maybe we'll do the picking after all."

"Wait. What? I thought it was up to me?"

They start to walk away, toward the parking lot. Then they turn and look over their shoulder, and say, "Maybe it's up to your past?"

But with a quick grab at the Chronosphere floating over their shoulder, they fling it high into the air.

And when it lands on the ground a second later, my whole world disappears in an explosion of light.

CHAPTER FIFTEEN

My dad used to let me sleep in, especially on the weekends. He'd say that sleep was super important to a creative mind, because things happen while we're in slumber. Our brain flushes out the bad chemicals, drowns itself in the good ones. Our dreams take us to foreign places and thoughts, and even through some dangerous territory—if we can remember them when we wake up.

He'd always start sketching on his notepad, one that he kept in his nightstand, the moment he opened his eyes, so things would stay fresh. Sometimes, he'd come up with the wildest things no one could ever envision awake, like the one time he drew a giraffe in rainbow-colored fishnet stockings. Totally weird and so not something my dad said he could ever come up with, but he knew that there are hidden chambers inside our bodies that can be unlocked, letting us discover wondrous things. And sometimes, what we find inside can help us make up our minds about whatever trouble we're facing.

Except all of that wonder inside me is gone. Each locker ransacked and emptied out. Not even my dreams bring me comfort anymore.

But I may be living an actual dream right now, because the Chronosphere is an unreality of its own. Twisted into a Möbius strip. Then dipped in panko and deep-fried.

There are a gazillion stairs and windows and doors in every direction around, above, and below me. Which doesn't make any sense at all, considering it's a tiny ball? And we're inside it somehow? "This . . . this all exists in that tiny glowing sphere?" I ask.

"'Tisn't your purpose to question, but to simply understand that it just is," Time says with a note of finality, as if this is not worth explaining. "Just accept it for what it is. All of time, all of the timeline, exists in here."

My mouth is positively agog, my eyes a-blinking rapidly at everything I can—"Wait, wait, wait a second. Just before we got in here, you mentioned something about my past?"

Time taps their chin. "Oh, did we finally get your attention with that very dramatic over-the-shoulder glance prior to our arrival? How do you like that truth serum now? See, don't you remember that you've given away your life to other people, not just your hamster or your granny. Several others have been the recipients of your accidental ability." Time holds up three fingers. "Specifically, this many."

"Uh, yes, I know about them . . ." But my tongue is now as useful as a car without wheels, while a window floats past, with random people from who-knows-where celebrating a birthday.

"Let's see," Time continues. "Someone named Holly. Then there's Yamany. Followed by a Jack."

It's as if my world has been thrown into a tumble-dryer and set to supersonic speed with those three names, my three friends . . . well, I used to call them friends. I guess it is true—that I'd accidentally given them life when I'd wished for them to be saved.

And it's now up to me to decide how to take those years back. Huge dry gulp here.

But as I watch a doorway fill with cries from a baby in a crib while her mother hovers over her, a massive question mark bonks me on the head. "So how much life did I actually give away?"

Time taps their knuckles, then pulls out their Chronosphere. "Well, each time you saved someone, you granted them twenty-two years. So technically, you were fine up until your nana."

"You're telling me I gave a hundred and ten years away and you did nothing about it?" I ask as a door saunters past—seriously, it's walking as if on legs—and from beyond it, the sounds of a roller-coaster along with the screams of dozens of terrified riders.

Time's eyebrows nearly knot together into an unknottable monobrow. "We are merely an accounting entity. But sometimes things run a little behind. Hence the accrual of your time debt. As with everything you're familiar with, tardiness is also a part of our timely constitution."

"So you're saying I'm supposed to live beyond a hundred?"

"No, that's not what we're saying."

"What're you saying then?"

"But we haven't said anything."

Ugh, this is so frustrating. "Can you just explain to me why the math is not adding up? Like, are there ridiculous medical advances in the future or something?" I stare at a window, at a woman wondering what to grab from the open door of a fridge. "Do I cryogenically freeze myself to extend my life?"

"Look. You will have the chance to live up to a certain number of years, which we shall not reveal. But we don't have to be mathing right now. Let's just say that you had given away too much. And now we have to take at least one of those gifts back."

The beeps of a ventilator in a hospital now, floating past me, through an open oak door. "So, I was supposed to live up to like a hundred-ish?"

There's a loud chittering in my bubble dome backpack, and Mary Shelley's mouth appears to be wide open, as if in shock.

"Again. We've not uttered a single word about years," Time says, turning away. Then they look over their shoulder. "Or have we? Either way, we are not in charge of how long you live. That, believe it or not, is up to you."

A hundred-ish years old. Golly. I guess this officially disproves my theory about Dad and me sharing the same fate. "You know what, I don't want to know how long I'm supposed to actually live."

And even if I take my years back, how am I going to go through life all by myself?

More than a hundred? Why would you want to be that old? Mary Shelley looks at me with so much questioning in her eyes.

All of this is very *Alice in Wonderland*, but very much real, not like that fiction of a story.

"I know, right? I don't even want to see the future that much," I say to her. "Do you?"

Then her attention turns to the pile of carrots on the shelf in the grocery store through the sliding glass door that's just appeared next to me.

Time casually points in the opposite direction at a wandering pond, then turns their attention back to me. "I say, if stress is a humanperson, it'd be you right now, especially with the way your whole body is tense like that," Time says with a flick of their short hair over their shoulders, which is obviously an utter fail. "We are going to one of the three undeservings, and you will simply have to pick who to undo your years for. That's it. That's all. Goodnight, folks."

Yikes. I try to think of a world without Jack or Yamany or Holly. Sadly, it doesn't look much different than my life for the last few months. But still. "I mean . . . I saved them for a reason. They were going to die."

"Goodness, were you the bearer of bad luck, or what? All these people around you almost dying. Yes, you did. But you can also unsave them."

"But doesn't that mean they will die immediately?"

"That's what taking life back means, yes."

"So you're saying I'm going to just effectively end things for them? For one of them?"

Time waves their hands next to their ears. "We swear we've been saying this very thing again and again. But why does it feel like it hasn't sunk in yet? Are you feeling a stint of déjà vu, because we certainly are. As in, 'Yes, that's what we've been saying, again and again.' This whole time. Also, since you've effectively failed at communicating with them, and by all accounts, they're no longer in your everyday vicinity, a 'hence' is very much in play here. As in, hence, we need to go to the past so you can make up your mind."

Revisiting my past with my three ex-friends is truly the last thing I want to do. But I don't see any other way to convince Time that there should be a loophole through all of this, that there should be a way out, that somehow I can make things work. "Can't I just take some of their years back. Like, enough from everyone to satisfy my debt?"

Time scratches their chin, pulls out the Chronosphere from their breast pocket, confers with it, then tucks it back in. "They say that rule hasn't been tested, but we can try."

Oh. I can decide that? But it'll also mean I have to decide how much value to place on their lives, and what they'll achieve in the future? Is that fair of me, to hold such power?

"Of course," Time continues. "Because it hasn't been tested, there's a chance all of them will expire in the process."

Okay, so maybe not as great of an option as I thought.

I have to figure this out. Time has mentioned multiple times that they are not human. And that's been very clear. But maybe that's where the solution lies. Time may have no emotions, but perhaps I can make them understand what it feels like to have to make these difficult decisions. To take even a day away from someone means potentially taking the happiest day from their life. But it could also be the saddest, most tragic one?

That's when I see a dark window, of an empty desert, without life. But something about it feels very apocalyptic, very . . . final.

Hmm.

Maybe I can show Time there's some worth to being human.

Maybe I can show them that we, as humankind, are worthy of being saved. Maybe if they understood that, they could find some excess time somewhere else to rescue us all without me giving up a single soul.

I don't know if it'll work, but I have to try. "If we're going to go on this journey, can you promise me that all my friends will be fine until I make my decision? Including Nana and Mary Shelley?"

"We thought you said the other three weren't your friends." Their eyes glow with something menacing.

It's at this very moment that I wonder, once again, if they are friend or foe.

I feel like I'm being forced to make a decision that will change all of humanity. And I am grossly unequipped. Someone who barely knows how to properly drive, who hasn't even left the comforts of his own city. So not well traveled like my dad or mom.

And that makes me wonder: What would either of them do, if given the chance to decide?

Well, I know my mom would make the rational decision, because that's what she has to do as a surgeon every single day in her career. She has to decide on one crucial, life-changing thing to save someone's life.

My dad, however, would look at everything as a whole, to see if all of it would fit together. And he'd say that sometimes, to make something beautiful, you have to start from scratch.

But that doesn't necessarily mean fixing things over and over again.

Wow. Does this mean . . . that he is here? No, I can't go there. I don't want to go there.

Back to what's important now. Maybe that's what this universe needs. Maybe we need to start from scratch. "What if we go back in time? All the way back to the beginning?"

Time cringes, their lips flattening into a thin line in an instant, their eyes going dull. "We don't think you'd like it much."

"Why?"

"Because there was nothing but us and the Chronosphere."

"Yikes. Wasn't that lonely?"

Time shrugs. "We don't understand what loneliness is because we have each other," they say, as they pull out the glittering gold ball again and let it float off their hand.

Why does that smell like a lie?

I can't help but give them the slyest side-eye. "So, you're not lonely then. Because you have the Chronosphere and me right now."

Time squints an eye. "We don't see you as being a part of any sort."

"Well, maybe we can go on this journey together."

"But we are going together."

Ugh. How do I make them understand? "Maybe I can show you everything about my past that can help you realize why this decision isn't easy." And my eyes go roving at the windows and doors around me, suddenly wondering how I can find myself amongst the billions or trillions of possibilities in here.

"We don't care about difficulty. We only care about saving the timeline," Time says.

"Yes, I know. Saving the timeline. You've said that a million times." This is going to be harder than I thought. "All right, if we're going on this journey, I'm taking Mary Shelley with me," I say, with a tap of my backpack.

Time rubs their hands and says, "Does this mean we're ready? Finally?"

My stomach sinks to my feet. I couldn't feel less ready to face this decision—or my past. But if my plan is going to work, I have no choice but to answer, "Yes."

CHAPTER SIXTEEN

Time says, "Now, let's go through what's you."

They flick a finger, and everything seems to reconfigure—as doors, stairs, windows, space and time, fly around in a frenzy. Yet Time and I remain a pair, an unmoving constant.

Seconds later, things settle down. And through every window and see-through door, I see an image of . . .

Me?

There's a loud but steady *cheet*. Mary Shelley's head is just spinning in every direction, as she gets more and more confused in her bubble dome backpack. *Where the hell are we and why'd you bring me here, because my head's about to pop off?*

There's baby me soon after birth in the hospital. With a trio of my mom and dad and a jubilant Nana all cooing down at the beautiful brown boy in his tiny crib.

Toddler me itching from chicken pox. Just hanging out in bed, with my mom. Just my mom. Which is kinda odd.

But who's that older man on a sailboat with wrinkles and eye-bags and the warm evening sun on his face, as he hugs another man I don't recognize from behind. Both of them with skins as brown as mine.

Wait. Is that last bit me, and my . . . future?

I can only watch as Future-Me grabs the hand of the other guy and plants a soft kiss on his palm, right on the spot of a faded scar that looks like a 7. Wow. They're so in love with each other, just the way they stare at each other. But who is this mystery man, and . . . when will I meet him?

I mean, there are so many me's.

Teen me on my bed alone, staring at his phone with a pout.

Seventy-ish me, with wrinkles all over, doing a marathon, with the finish line a hundred yards away.

Forty-ish me, looking quite dashing, wining and dining with friends. Lots of laughs being had.

Sixty-ish me looking at a relatively healthy bank statement. Yes, that number looks quite comfortable to retire on, even as he finds himself in a modestly sized house quite like the one I live in.

Twenty-ish me in college. Staring intensely at his professor going on about how to plot a novel.

Which is . . . yeah. I can't even begin to describe it. I currently am in a personal universe of me, as in, I'm directly in the center of it all. Which is a jarring concept to even try to comprehend.

Because I remember my dad telling me that it's all about ego. We all have one, and it's hard to not think of our *self* when thinking about others' selves. But we have to be aware of who we are before we can think about others. He didn't do a great job of explaining it well—I was only twelve at the time—but his message was that, ultimately, to be able to care for others means to care for who we are, and selflessness is only attainable after we're in complete understanding of our limitations, or, just like a candle, we'll eventually burn out.

Which, in this case, as I witness a million me's in all configurations of history and future and events I can't even imagine going through—is that me skydiving with gray hair?!—makes me feel smaller than a grain of salt.

"What . . . where . . . *when* do we go?" I ask.

Time stuffs their hands into the pockets of their neon-orange jumpsuit and clicks the heels of their flats. "You tell us. You want moment of conception? Birth? Death? Well, maybe not death, since that'll spoil things a little. How about a trial run?"

Uh, I don't know where to start. I am curious about that sailboat, but I don't know if I'm willing to find out what my future has in store for me. "Sure?"

They walk over to a plain tan door, twist the silver knob, and swing it open. "Right through here."

A quick peek: it looks like my bedroom.

I step on through and am instantly transported to . . . yeah, it's my room.

But even without being told when in time we've gone, I know. The clues are there.

The messy desk. An odor of unwashedness that's kinda like a Brie left out in the open for a week. And the hunchbacked me— Past-Me—who sits there, staring at his laptop screen, with absolutely nothing on it.

A twinge twists my stomach. "This was a month after my dad died. This was when I first did the impossible. Without even realizing it."

The older and unimproved Present-Me takes a careful step forward, so I can watch over the shoulder of Past-Me. I can't help but swallow the lump growing in my throat. Because the memory of what he's about to come face-to-face with suddenly rips a torrent through my mind.

Sure enough, there she is. Mary. My poor hamster.

Another *cheet* coming from my chest. *Oh goodness gracious. Was that . . . me?*

I can only nod. "You don't have to watch this if you don't want to."

She's lying on her side, on the desk, barely breathing. But instead of being covered in snow-white fur, this younger version is a creamy chocolate. Her eyes are closed, her breaths so slow and shallow that the both of us have to freeze for several heartbeats, to see the tiny fraction of an inch her chest will rise. Every breath taking a half second longer than the one before.

Mary is dying. (Again, to me.)

Past-Me can only stare at her, all sense of defeat suffused over his slumped body.

Mary opens her eyes once. Maybe for the last time. *Wow. Never thought breathing could be this hard. And honestly, I've never felt this tired before. My whole body is just . . . weary. And all I ever did was run that wheel.*

"Are you okay?" I say to Mary Shelley, as she looks on at Mary, her former self.

The chittering on my chest calms down. *I do have to say, it's nice to be able to actually breathe properly again now. Old me had it pretty rough back then.*

"I don't know why I named her Mary, and I don't know why I loved the name. Maybe because it was such a simple one," I say to Time, who stays back at the doorway. I don't know what makes me say it, but I guess the little things are what come to mind when you're about to lose someone you love.

And here we are, waiting for Mary's final breaths.

At precisely fifteen hundred and three hours, the old hamster seems to let out one final wheeze. *I think this is it. You've been a wonderful, even if a bit morose at times, friend.*

A squirm ripples its way through my gut. Finally realizing those were Mary's actual last words. (Even if they were in my mind.)

Eventually, a previously wordless Past-Me says, ever so calmly, "I can't lose you, too, Mary."

"This is the moment," I say to Time. "This is when it happens."

Past-Me stares out the window at the kids playing on the street. As if they've swallowed all the happy pills in the world. And he wonders if he'll ever experience that kind of joy ever again. "I just wish I could save you."

Nothing.

"Please, just come back. I'll do anything."

Still nothing.

A deep breath later, Past-Me goes, "I wish you could stay with me forever, Mary. Can you imagine? All the fun we would have. I'd even take you traveling all around the world if I could. If only you could stay alive until my final breathing hours."

Mary is still. Unmoving.

Finally, after a bit of quiet, he'll say the words. And he doesn't even know he's saying it, or if anyone will hear it, but he wants his own ears to bear witness to them floating in the quiet air of his bedroom, rather than be choked by the roil of his insides.

He lets out a sigh. "Just until I turn thirty-nine."

And the change happens within a second of the period at the end of that sentence.

Mary's chest rises and falls dramatically, as if someone's just pumped her full of oxygen. Her beady black eyes pop open, and she props herself up onto her tiny paws. Then she gives Past-Me the strangest look. *How did you do what you did and what just happened to me? It's funny because I thought I was falling asleep and I was going to be dreaming, but I snapped right back. No dream or whatever.*

Although Past-Me blinks as much as Mary does, before gasping and letting out a strangled, "Oh my God, Mary. How? What? Why? I thought I'd lost you." He carefully lays a hand down, and Mary climbs into it, gnawing at his thumb—maybe to test out if all of what she's going through is real.

Past-Me obviously can't believe his luck. Their luck, actually. "Wow. This is a miracle. Should I call you Mary Shelley now? Because I think you've just Frankensteined yourself out of death."

He lowers his face to hers and nuzzles her head on his cheek.

While I can only stare at these two figures, before uttering a strangled, "I had no idea that could happen. I didn't think I was responsible for it, not then. All I could think of was, it must have been wishful thinking. A coincidence."

I had no idea I was capable of something wondrous.

Time, who'd stayed at the entrance to the room, simply raises a hand and says, "We wouldn't call it wondrous. It was—"

I turn to the imposing figure. "Stop intruding on my thoughts. Okay, it was magical, then. Can you also just let me believe for once that I had a superpower?"

Time merely shrugs. "Well, what is a superpower if not an ability of extraordinary nature. Much like the human who could hold their breath underwater for ten minutes, much longer than most others on the planet."

Past-Me grabs a dry carrot stick and hands it to the new and zombifyingly improved Mary Shelley's suddenly greedy paws.

I take a step back and watch the pair, content in their new life together. But also bewilderment. Because I realize this is only the beginning, as I look down at the curious hamster on my chest. "So I did give twenty-two, maybe twenty-three, years to Mary Shelley?"

She's lying on her side now, as if she's about to smoke a cigar, seemingly content at watching her own resurrection. *I guess you did.*

"Yes, you did." Time says, filing their nails with a sheet of sandpaper that's materialized out of nowhere. "See how the math is starting to math up?"

CHAPTER SEVENTEEN

I can only stare at the sandpaper in Time's hand, which disappears with my look, as we once again stand around back in the Chronosphere, with its many windows, stairs, and doors. "I guess I can call this the . . . 'Chronolobby'?"

"Shall we start getting serious now?" Time ignores my comment as they tap furiously at their wrist. "We think this gesture means we need to speed things up before our hand drops off our arm bone?"

"Ugh, fine. As if seeing my hamster dying once again wasn't traumatic." I give her a quick glance. I mean, it sure was, but getting to see her re-resurrection was an eerily joyful moment, too, if there's such a thing. "Where do we go?"

"You mean 'When do we go?' You'll see."

They flick a finger, and the Chronosphere reconfigures. Doors, stairways, windows shifting and flying as a loud *whir* fills the entire space, causing my eyes to flutter at the confusing blur.

"Believe me, this is a lot easier than running up and down stairs to find the one door out of a trazillion just to get to the moment we need to get to, don't you think?" Time says. "But here's the door, right here." They walk over to one made of stout oak and slide it to one side.

Oh no. Oh God no. "You've taken me to him, haven't you?"

"Of course we have. We have to do this. You know, we have to make sure we check out each of the candidates."

Oh Lord, why do we have to do this now? Especially after all I've gone through with him. But if I want to save the timeline, it's time to get serious, I guess.

We're outside the open door to an apartment, as a couple of my schoolmates walk up and casually enter, carrying a six-pack among them. It's on the top floor of the four-story building I know so well.

Time snaps their fingers and we're instantly transported inside.

"This is where Jack lives," I say, taking in the familiar scene. "But his dad was away visiting his mom in Yemen. So he's by himself, but he's invited all his friends over, and things got a little out of hand."

"Which one is he? Point him out to us? We want to see," Time says with glee. "Also, why does it smell all chemical in here? Almost like musk?"

"Oh, it's all of us teens in one space, I guess?" The clock on the wall above the couch says 9:47. I know where we were supposed to be at this point.

Right there, on the balcony. Just the two of us, as everyone's in the living room watching a pair of our classmates bitch about our homeroom teacher.

With a snap of Time's fingers, we're transported again to the fresh Los Angeles air of outside. Jack and Past-Me are both in the middle of some funny anecdote.

Ugh. I don't even remember the last time I felt whatever *he* was feeling.

"Sooo," Time asks. "What was going on with the two of you?"

My face must look like it's been swallowed by the sun, as heated as it is. "What do you mean? We were friends. Nothing more."

"No clue what that means. What's more than friends? Why do you look at him the way you do? Like you're in desperate need of water?" Time asks, with an odd expression, something unseen before.

Looking at Past-Me, it's . . . yeah. Obvious. Only my crush is the oblivious one in all of this. Even an immortal being with no emotions can see what is so clearly written all over my face.

Jack and Past-Me face each other, leaning against the parapet. They've just finished laughing at the story they're sharing with each other. And they've moved on to something more serious.

"Are you sure you want to try it?" Jack asks. "Like, really, really sure?"

Past-Me's breathing gets a little heavy, his pupils dilating. "Yeah, why not?"

There's a pause as his gaze drops. Going down down down. Hip-level.

"It can be kinda hard to swallow," Jack says. "For a virgin."

I can't help but roll my eyes as I turn to Time. "Good Lord.

Listen to these two and their chat bait. Makes me want to puke so hard. What the hell was I thinking?"

Then it's Past-Me's turn to roll his eyes as he grabs the bottle of Bud Light from Jack's hand. "I figure it's time to get started with this drunking thing that everyone's so obsessed with. Might as well go big." Without another second's delay, he tips it back, taking a huge chug, and almost sputters it out, before his entire face folds up. "Oh, is that what regret tastes like?"

Mary Shelley's squirming around in the backpack. *All the baby carrots are about to spew out in a gooey orangey mess.*

I can only give her a look. "Calm down. We weren't that bad."

Time can only shrug. "They look like they adore unnecessary chitchat."

"You didn't even give me a chance to distract you." Jack grins, with a naughty glint in his eyes. "I would've told you a joke or something."

Past-Me grimaces at the second, more conservative sip and nearly chokes. "Does it get any better?"

Jack's eyes lose the tiniest bit of their glimmer, even as the smile stays. "If you keep drinking, the world actually starts to look better, I promise."

I can only sigh as I watch this mismatched pair. "I don't know why the old Jack kept thinking his world was ever going to improve. Because I don't think it ever will. Not with his dad the way he is."

But Past-Me looks down at his feet and asks his friend, "Are you doing okay?"

Jack turns to the mountains silhouetted against the dark and shrugs. His body language says everything. "I think eventually I'll get through it. Is this what they mean by having 'daddy issues'?"

"Ugh, speaking of issues. I still haven't cried. And it's been a whole month," Past-Me confesses. "My dad would say it's a huge problem, if he was still alive. Do you think that's a problem with us boys? Or do you think it's a problem with them men?"

Jack shrugs again. "I don't cry because my dad would beat the hell out of me if I did. And you don't cry because you haven't figured out how to yet. Because *when* exactly is the right time?"

Past-Me remains silent at this.

While I just stand here, watching both of them, wondering, *When?* And why his words sound so true.

"Hey, I'm gonna grab a few more for us, and then we'll go up to the roof," Jack says.

So they leave the balcony and make their way into the kitchen.

Time watches. "Something going on between the two of you out there. How do you—"

"Hush now," I say, with a finger on my lips, but not quite rudely. "There was nothing going on between the two of us. We were just the closest friends. Known each other since middle school. And—"

"Hush now. Let's find out what happens," Time interrupts with a finger to their lips and a side-eye.

Before I can balk at the rudeness, they snap their fingers, and . . . Poof.

We're on the roof. And I'm right behind my history.

Two boys lying on a blanket, watching the sky, with a Bud Light in each of their hands. Both wrapped up in a cloud of sudden giggles.

Once Past-Me breaks into character again, he says, "Oh God. Is this how it feels to be drunk? Why do I feel like the stars are spinning, and in a really good way? Oh, also does it feel like we should plan a rave or something? By the way, what actually is a rave? Is it when you give five-star reviews on an app after you watch someone perform on stage?"

Jack finally settles down, too. "You've only had three beers. I don't know if that's considered drunkenness. Although, since it's your first time, maybe you are. But wait until you wake up tomorrow."

Past-Me gasps. "Is the hangover thing really real? Like, is my head going to feel like someone's split it in half with an axe?"

Jack grimaces, then grins a fake grin at the sky. "If you keep drinking water, like really stuff yourself to the point where you're almost a merman, then maybe you'll be fine after all. But don't say I didn't warn you."

There's a quiet moment, where they share a look and something unspoken. And my heart yearns for them to just address it. Talk about it. Whisper to someone about it.

I look down, suddenly overcome by shyness. But Mary Shelley's beaming up at me, in the weirdest way ever. *You're a romantic, aren't you?*

"Shush. You don't know what you're talking about."

But all Past-Me says is, "I'm sorry about you and your dad. I wish there was something I could do about it. Like, let you stay in our guest house."

Jack swats away the sympathy. "Nah, I don't want to cause any trouble. You know I'm used to living here alone. My dad's got to do his thing, and my mom's got no interest in coming back here. So, it's whatever, you know? Besides, going solo isn't all that bad. I've learned to not get depressed about it."

Past-Me scoffs. "I doubt it. Bet you watch porn like twenty-four-seven. Or at least, when you're not in school."

It's Jack's turn to scoff. "What do you mean? I'm an angel."

Ugh, stop with the teasing already. Good Lord, these two could make a nunnery look like a red-light district. How I wish I could cut the tension and eliminate all teasing between them eleven months ago. All they had to do was just figure out what they were both into.

All I had to do was ask him if he was into . . . me?

"Hey, do you think we'll ever be happy?" Past-Me asks.

Jack's silent for more than a moment. To the point where it's a little awkward, as if he'd fallen asleep and was near-snoring. "Who knows, Haz. We're both not even adults yet. Sometimes I have to remind myself that's how young I am, because it feels like I'm being thrown into adulthood, without my approval. But eventually we'll have to grow up. And if we don't figure out how to be happy now, I don't think we ever will."

"Ugh, why do you sound so cool and wise for a drunkie?"

"I'm not trying at all. Haven't you realized I'm just naturally cooler than you are?" he says as he takes a chug from his bottle.

"I think you have a drinking problem, because you're obviously too drunk and talking nonsense. Oh wait, maybe I'm the one with a drinking problem, because I'm really liking how this feels." Past-Me punctuates that silliness with a hiccup.

I recall now, even with my current sobriety, the surge of something that felt like courage after all that drink. I've never wanted to confess my feelings to Jack, but at that moment, under the dim stars and smoggy LA sky, having sipped several audacity ales, the desire to do something really stupid was pushing me to the edge.

I was feeling all sorts of brave.

Jack pulls himself up, leans back on his hands, his gaze out at the dark horizon.

Past-Me stares at the boy with the most beautiful face. Even in the dim light.

I do, too, but from the opposite side, a totally different angle, but he's still beautiful nonetheless.

Breathtaking even.

The moment suddenly felt magical.

"Don't do it," I say, as I creep over to the other side, within inches of Past-Me's ear. "Please, just . . . forget it. Leave him alone. So you don't destroy your friendship."

Time screams out with their hands clutching their hips. "You can't change him. You can't change anything in here. Think of it as a replay. Of moments gone by. We can even rewind a little if you want?"

"Leave me alone, please," I say, rather rudely this time. It's embarrassing enough knowing what they're about to witness. I don't need their commentary, too.

Time doesn't look the slightest bit offended. They're merely standing there, taking in the whole situation.

Past-Me brings himself up to the same level, with the same pose. "Don't go jumping off the roof. I promise you won't bounce or fly off the edge." Then a little quieter, and a lot less funny: "Besides, I can't lose my best friend."

He's staring straight into Jack's eyes.

God, my heart was like a trapped bird, beating its wings so hard, trying to escape its cage, so it could fly free.

Past-Me will not understand what is about to happen. Because he has too much adrenaline and liquid courage burning through his veins, making him feel more alive than ever before.

But . . .

Stars + dark night sky + just the two of them + no one around + Bud Light = the ripest and most perfect moment.

So Past-Me leans in. Leans in real hard. And says, "Jack, I love you."

The boy's head makes the sharpest turn that could blur any video taken of the moment. He smiles, but with a blush. "Oh, you know I love you, too, Hazeem. You're my best friend."

Then he leans into Past-Me with a hug, but the moment their faces are an inch apart, Past-Me leans in again and tries to kiss him.

Jack instantly pulls away. Looks almost disgusted, a sneer on his face.

That's all he does before he gets up and storms off, holding on tight to the beer bottle in his hand.

Mary Shelley's cleaning her paws. *Wow, you really killed that moment, didn't you?*

CHAPTER EIGHTEEN

My entire body has shriveled up to the size of a grape from all the cringing. Seriously, I'm just a head, arms, and legs at this point.

We watch Jack try to make a hasty retreat in the dark of the roof.

"It wasn't too bad, was it?" I ask.

Mary Shelley's scratching at the bubble dome, looking for attention. *Define "bad," because what I've just witnessed is the equivalent of a supervolcano rising up and drowning the entire planet with an oceanful of lava.*

Time chuckles, then smooths their face at my glare. "The rodent's not too bad, after all."

But Past-Me is already scrambling after his love-of-the-moment to try and make things right. "Jack, I'm so sorry. I just . . . I don't know what came over me. I'm just drunk. That's all."

Jack's too busy trying to figure out which way is which, before turning around, and grabbing the blanket, folding it clumsily with one hand, clutching tightly to the Bud Light. "I don't want to talk about it, Haz. I'm . . . I'm tired. I'm going to tell everyone to go home."

"You don't have to do that. Can we just pretend like it never happened?" Past-Me begs.

Jack merely scoffs. "Look, I need to get some sleep. Clearly you do, too. We'll talk tomorrow. Okay?"

Every part of me aches as I watch the scene unfold. Because I can't stop what's about to happen.

Past-Me takes a step forward, closer to Jack.

He takes a step back. "No, Haz."

"Look, this isn't me," Past-Me says. "I obviously can't think straight right now."

Jack sneers again, and he doesn't seem to believe a single word of what Past-Me said. It was a new facial expression then, but now it's the only one he wears any time I'm near him. I seem to be the only reason he's ever looked like that.

Time starts fanning their face. "Whoa. we're getting so hot and worked up from watching this drama unfold. But the two of you need to take a course on how chemistry works, because this fizzling isn't exactly it. Seriously, it's like taking a shower with hydrochloric acid—it just burns, doesn't it? But what exactly did you do to him?"

I can only watch as Jack continues to keep his distance, as he continues to argue with Past-Me.

"I tried to kiss him," I explain to Time. "It was so stupid. But

I was drunk and he was my best friend and I . . . I loved him." It feels strange to say that part out loud. "There was probably, definitely a more courageous way to tell the boy I loved most in the world about my feelings for him, but that night, the alcohol made me put it all on display."

Time shakes their head, then pulls out the Chronosphere. "Wow. We can only guess what this courage thing is, because it seems like yours got a strong reaction out of him based on what's happening right now. And not in a good way."

The voices from the argument keep going up by three decibels with every single sentence that's being spat out, but it's obvious Jack has stopped listening.

I can't stand to watch, so I refocus on my overall mission and try once again to explain a human concept to an immortal being. "Courage is about finding strength," I say to Time. "It's trying to figure out a way to make it through something, to summon the strength to do something you've never done before or are scared of. No, that doesn't make any sense at all, as I listen to myself say it. I don't know how else to explain it, though. I guess one day I will just have to show you."

Time snickers, while showing all of their teeth. "One day? We don't know if that will ever happen, will it? Someday? Tomorrow? The near future? Those are whens that currently hang in the balance because someone is refusing to figure out what to do about it."

I can only cross my arms across the bubble dome backpack, as I hang my head. Because suddenly it feels like I'm being attacked by both Time and Jack.

Looking down, I'd forgotten Mary Shelley's watching along. *Wow, no wonder Jack stopped talking to you. You didn't even ask him if you could kiss him. That's a big no, Haz.*

"Ugh, I know, Mary Shelley."

It wasn't just the consent thing, though. It was all much bigger than that. Eleven months ago, and within the timespan of two minutes, Jack went from being my best friend to just somebody that I used to know. We used to hang out practically every day. He would tell me everything about his dad and I would tell him everything about my dad, but ever since this moment on the roof, he'd decided that was all over. That I was no longer going to be a part of his life.

I don't even know what to think anymore.

But I know this is when the magic happens. Or is that the curse?

I can barely turn to look at the both of them.

Time merely claps their hands, which sounds like a crack of thunder. "Oh, look, look, look. I think we're getting closer and closer. Or, *he* is."

Because it's true. Jack's been retreating—creating as much space between himself and Past-Me—to the point where he's a single foot away from the edge of the roof. And Past-Me just doesn't realize it, both of them too drunk to stop the tragedy that's about to unfold.

But before Past-Me can say one more word, Jack simply raises his hands to the high heavens and screams, "Just leave me alone." He takes one final step back.

All he finds is air underneath his foot. And himself tumbling backward. Letting go of the steady ground, and the Bud Light in his hand.

And there is nothing Past-Me can do to stop it.

Both boys can only stare at each other, as time decays into sticky molasses, into a sickening sort of slow motion.

Past-Me rushes forward with arms outstretched, in the space of a half second while screaming his head off. Trying to figure out a way to stop the potentially terminal fall from four floors up.

Because he can't have someone else die in his life, even as he screams, "Nooooooo!"

But Jack continues to fall, craning his neck up, eyes round and large, full of disbelief at his final moments alive.

And Past-Me remembers. The image of Mary Shelley flashing bright, with the loudest fireworks going off in his head. All those words he said, and the only ones that seemed to work.

Something inside him wells up into a ball of energy, and he subconsciously says, "Twenty-two years."

That was it. Just like that.

"What?" Time says with a squinty eye. "Just like that? Just like that. How easyfied."

Past-Me teeters over the edge, ignoring the number of beers he's had.

I creep along with Time to stand near Past-Me, and we stare over the lip of the roof.

The smash of a glass bottle resounds from hitting the asphalt down below—but with not much else.

And the most bewildering sight takes hold of Past-Me. He'll remember seeing it back then, but he's definitely too drunk to understand what's happening.

Because there is a floating Jack below all of us.

Looking up at Past-Me with arms windmilling, but he's also

trying to gain purchase since he's only three feet off the ground. Swimming in a stewy gumbo of air and shadows and dim starlight.

But eventually, one foot taps the ground, then the other, then both hands, as he lands on his haunches before steadying himself.

Jack drops to his knees, and stays there. Then he spends another second creakily staring up, but without really understanding how, although he has a good measure of pain on his face, as if he's wincing at what he sees.

But his eyes glaze over with the final ebbs of alcohol burning away the adrenaline in his veins, and that same sneer creeps back in.

He finally turns to walk away.

Leaving his ex-best friend—leaving me—behind.

CHAPTER NINETEEN

'Tis better to have lost. And I indeed did that night. What I knew then was that I'd lost the boy I loved, the one who'd always trusted me to be his friend. But what I didn't know was that I'd also lost twenty-two years of my own life.

Which meant by then, I'd lost more than forty years already, counting what I gave Mary Shelley. Goddammit. Such a long time squandered away.

But it's entirely possible that if I hadn't given those years away, they might've been ultimately filled with emptiness. And seeing how alcohol had something to do with that night, I'm surprised it wasn't linked with how I felt, leading me down a dark road of lonely nights filled only with the loud chugs of—

Okay, I'm just glad Bud Light tasted horrible enough for me to not want to have another sip of it after that devastating incident. So at least one good thing came out of it?

But there's no way I can take those years back from this boy. Even after all that's happened.

I'd carved him out of my heart, leaving behind a Jack-shaped empty space. A space that I won't have any more time to fill it up with.

"Well, well, well," Time says. "Look at all the stars so many light-years away from us. But isn't it odd that they're not twinkling at all? Not one bit. It's almost as if their ability to burn their gas off has been . . . frozen. Stopped in time. Because someone," and this is when they turn to me, "has decided to become the only star worth shining in our entire existence."

"Why are you pressuring me?" I say with puffy cheeks. "You just saw everything. Jack almost died! I couldn't just let that happen. I barely even understood what I was doing. I don't know how this magic works."

"Magic? Magic, as in stuff that happens outside of normal scientific explanations and calculations? That was not magic. That was *time*. Well, time molecules to be exact."

"Wait, you know how this is all happening?" I ask. "Why didn't you say anything before?"

Time shrugs. "Didn't seem relevant."

I take a deep breath to keep from screaming. "Well, I find it very relevant. Can you explain? Please?"

"Fine. All that time you spent sitting comatose in your room caused something extraordinary to take place—the mutation of your allotted time molecules. See, you spent so much time hyperfixating on this ridiculous idea of living only till you turn thirty-nine, that it altered the bonds of those molecules in such a way that allowed them to detach from you, which then gave you the ability to simply give them away. You didn't seem interested in using them, so they gladly transferred to other beings. That was what you did with that boy. It was the same thing you did with Mary Shelley. But you doing all that was the first time anything of this sort has ever happened, however. And we shall make sure it won't happen again. Now, why you would ever give up your time, especially when that boy almost died trying to get *away* from you, is beyond our comprehension."

Ugh. Something continues to carve a hole out of my chest, really trying to empty out my insides, leaving behind a massive black hole. I'm the exact opposite from being the bright shining star Time is trying to brand me as. "I did it because he's the love of my life."

Wait. Did I just say that out loud? Is Jack the love of my life? I mean, I do love him, but is he that? Even when he refuses to have anything to do with me? Sounds super depressing when I think of it like that, actually.

Time surprises me with what they say next. "What is love?"

Ack. I take it all back, seriously all of it, even my self-confession at being so deeply in love—I mean, in emotions, for Jack. *How should I know?* is the first thing that pops into my mind. Because the L word is truly impossible to describe, isn't it? I know it's a strong feeling, especially what I felt for my dad, and what happened after his death was that feeling started to decay, to rot away, into anguish and tons of sorrow, and lying around . . . which apparently got me into this mess. I think my definition of that very intense word has waned into some foreign, strange concept.

111

But then I look down at my bubble dome backpack. My little friend has been so quiet, just watching everything that's transpired. *Don't look at me. I'm just here for the drama.*

"Love is . . ." I try to explain, but nothing concrete comes to me. Jack's face—smiling, not sneering—flashes in my mind. And I hate that for me. "Oh my gosh, do I have to teach you everything?"

Time's face is utter blankness. Totally unreadable. As smooth as plain paper. "You have to understand that these are all foreign concepts to us. We don't understand a single thing about human stuff. So tell us what is this love thing, and why are you all so obsessed with it? It's almost as if you use it to justify every single reason for everything that you do. And apparently because it was what you confessed to that boy. So, tell us."

I run my hands over my face, trying to wipe away my earlier annoyance. It's a fair question—I just don't want to answer it. "Uh . . . it's this . . . it's kind of embarrassing. Okay, so love is a strong desire, an emotion, something intense. Honestly, I'm clueless about how to explain what it is, exactly."

"Well, talk about it scientifically."

I think about Nana, Mary Shelley, my dad (again), also my mom. Try to come up with words to describe the feeling in my brain, my body, my metaphorical heart. "There's no scientific explanation to it. I guess, by all accounts and from what I've heard, it's a chemical reaction in your brain—dopamine, endorphins, that kind of thing. But there's more to it than that. Something mystical. Spiritual."

"We don't understand those words. Only the scientifical, theoretical, factual."

112

How do I make them understand? "Love happens as you create a bond with someone that can never be broken apart. Ever."

Time shakes their head again. "We don't understand bonds other than those of an atomic nature. Like time molecules."

"Okay then, so take the bonds inside one of those. Imagine how the protons are so attracted to the nucleus that they can't be easily pulled apart. Their bonds cannot be broken easily. I guess that could be an easy way to describe love, or at least attraction. It's this intense feeling for someone that makes you feel like it'll kill you if anyone or anything tries to rip you two apart."

Time grits their teeth, makes a wheezing noise. "Sounds rather stalkery, don't you think? Well, let's just take a look at what happens to your love for that Jack. Shall we?"

With a sudden snap of their fingers we're back in the Chronosphere and careening through a door made out of water.

"We're going to see some Fast Futures following that canceled deathfall," Time says.

There's Past-Me, the day after, in my bedroom, lying, staring at the ceiling. An air of moroseness clouds the room. Coupled with a light stench of not giving a damn.

The phone next to him must have been scratched from those stunted fingernails, from Past-Me's thumb constantly checking for messages and notifications.

But Jack has not responded to a single one.

Time yanks me out, then, through another watery door.

Nausea grabs my throat, but I pry its clammy fingers away. I can do this.

It's two days later, and Past-Me is at Jack's doorstep knocking furiously, but when he peers through the blinds, there's just a shadow there, hovering around. As if ignoring everything going on outside his apartment.

Time drags me by the shoulder, back out, and through another watery doorway still.

Three days later.

And finally, a text message.

Past-Me stares at it.

My dad's back. So I don't think it's a good idea. Sorry I've been quiet but I'll talk to you when I can.

I scoff seeing the message now. "Yeah, right," I say.

"What do you mean, 'yeah, right'? He did the exact opposite," Time very helpfully points out. "He hasn't tried talking to you ever since then, even though you saved his life."

"It's called sarcasm," I explain, knowing they probably won't understand. "I guess I can't blame him though. Why couldn't he be more like Ned, you know, so gung ho about his best friend—Spider-Man—being a superhero? Instead, Jack chose to cut me off. Some friend."

Time's eyes grow wide, as if they're suddenly interested to be taking in all this information. "And is there anything you'd like to tell us, maybe? About him? And about your decision for him?"

Ugh. I can't do this now. "I just . . . I know he was going through a lot. And his dad wasn't the best." But a thought strikes me. "Hey, I'm kind of curious. Do you think we can go back to the past, to not look at me?"

"What do you mean?" Time asks.

I don't know if they'll go for it. Because it may feel like we're bending the rules a little. "I mean, can I take a look at *his* past?"

Time pipes up. "Ooh. A sneak attack. We like. Let's do it."

CHAPTER TWENTY

Time claps their hands with an indescribable feverishness. "But of course we can grant your pair of squishy socket meats a chance to feast their gaze at anything that happens in the timeline. Is this what you need to help cement your decision?"

We're just wandering around the inside of the Chronosphere. But it's obvious they'll only help me if it gets us to the correct outcome. "Um, yeah, there was this one incident with Jack." Gosh. It's been killing me, trying to figure it out. Maybe a little bit of spying won't actually hurt?

Mary Shelley looks at me with wide eyes. *You're really asking to be punished hard, aren't you?*

"Ignoring you, and thanks for the unwanted advice." But I go on. "We were texting one night. Six months before he stopped talking to me. He had a huge argument with his dad. And we were going back and forth, super easy and super flowy, but at one point, he was typing and deleting and typing and deleting . . . but that was all I could see. I just want to know what he was trying to say."

This memory has stuck in my head because it was around this time I could have sworn friendship turned to something . . . more? Maybe I was just seeing what I wanted to see, but I've always wondered if this moment could have changed everything for the better before I changed it all for the worst.

Time gives a salute, as they roll up the sleeves of their orange jumpsuit. "Of course, let's do that."

There's a giant, echoing, sucking noise . . .

And Time reconfigures the stairs, doors, and windows. Until all I see is Jack.

My heart plunges in an instant at seeing his face once again. Those sharp cheekbones. Those warm brown eyes. Why am I still feeling this way?

I peer through all the doors and windows and come across that one moment.

So we hop into his living room.

There he is. Having the biggest argument with his dad.

"I don't want to hear it!" his dad yells. "It is your duty to carry on our name—to marry a nice girl and have a son. *That* is your future. You are going to Yemen. Your mother and I will find some-one for you. End of discussion."

But Jack just shakes his head, unwilling to listen to another word. "No, Dad, I want to live here. I'm not just going to do whatever you want me to!"

"You're a *child*! You don't know what you're thinking." His dad's whole face shakes as he speaks. "I know what's best for you.

Do you think your mother was happy here? Hmm? Do you think it's easy taking care of you by myself? It's only because of my job that we can all survive!"

Jack sighs out of frustration, scratching at his neck as a tiny bit of anger leaves his body. "I know, I know. I know that. But you can't just expect me to give up my entire life. I have friends. I have everything here! I don't know Yemen!"

"Then it's time you get to know it." His father's quiet voice reverberates across the room. "Your mother and I came to America because we were hypnotized by the dream of a better life, especially when she found out she was pregnant with you. To have something safer, more stable, to surround you with books we didn't have. But our chase for money has led us to hate everything around us. Why do kids have to wear bulletproof backpacks here? Why are we still being called names? Why do I make less than all the other mechanics I work with even though I've been there fifteen years?"

Jack's shoulders slump. Maybe he's starting to understand what his dad's been going through the entire time he's been living in this foreign country.

His dad finally sighs, goes to the fridge to grab a Bud Light, then returns, crashing into the couch. "I will not discuss it any further with you. You are coming with me. I'm making plans already. One more year and then we are done here."

"That is not fair. I still have to finish school. I still have to go to college."

"You can continue university in Yemen." There's a note of finality to these words, something Jack isn't allowed to question. "Besides I have nothing left for me here other than you. Both sides of our family are back there. So this is the best decision I can make for us."

Jack's very clearly lost the argument.

So he runs off, away from his overbearing dad, and into his bedroom, slamming the door shut and flinging himself onto his twin bed.

He stares out the window, his eyes vacant, as if deep in thought.

I knew Jack and his dad fought. He had told me how strained their relationship was, how this was the worst fight they'd ever had, but he didn't tell me all the details.

"I wish he would have told me everything," I find myself saying. "If I had known . . ."

Time merely chuckles. "You wouldn't have known, would you? Because to us, it looks like you weren't the greatest of friends after all. You weren't enough of a best friend to him and he wasn't enough of a best friend to you."

"Don't say that!" I say, louder than I expected. I take a deep breath, then let it out gently, to remind myself that Time is doing this on purpose to try and get me to take my years back from Jack. "You don't know him like I do. He was the bestest friend anyone could ever have."

Jack grabs his phone from the nightstand and stares at the screen. This is when he starts texting me, trying to tell me tiny bits about what just happened. That his dad wanted him to go back to Yemen. But he didn't say why.

There's a twisting in my gut. I can't imagine how it would feel to be forced to marry someone I didn't know and didn't love. I know arranged marriages happen in so many places around the world. But I'd like to have a say in who I spend the rest of my life with.

And Jack deserves the same. The direction of our lives should be driven by our own hands. And looking at Jack's sad face, it sucks knowing that even though he's almost an adult, he still doesn't have a say in what would happen to him.

The boy is silently tapping on the phone.

And I peer over his shoulder, waiting to see the message he was struggling to send.

He types:

I don't want to leave

Then a video call comes in, interrupting him. He answers. "Mom?"

A woman's face appears, eyebrows knotted, hair in a bun. "Yaacob. What did you say to your father?"

Jack rolls his eyes. "Nothing. But he said you both want me to move back to Yemen. And I don't know if I want to."

His mom shakes her head. "Do you really want to stay there when there's no one? No family?"

"I did have family here. I had you here," Jack says. Then more quietly, "At least . . . until six years ago. Why'd you have to leave? We could've been good here."

She stares off-screen, her eyes suddenly going vacant.

I watch this interaction with a slimy queasiness in my stomach. This feels voyeuristic, because he's spoken very little about his mom before. He'd just say that she left and went back to Yemen.

But she continues. "I tried. Believe me, I did. I just couldn't feel at home. America to me felt like a factory: you clock in, make your money, gossip with some of your coworkers, and when you're ready, you clock out. Leave, and never look back. There was no community. No *life*."

119

"I'm sorry you felt that way, Mom. But that's not how I feel about this place at all. I do have a community—I have friends."

This time she laughs, and it touches her distant eyes. "Of course, you young ones feel that way. But when you get to my age, you value family, and I missed mine. I miss you too dearly, of course. You are my only child. But America . . . it wasn't good for me. You know, it got to the point where I became so afraid, I couldn't even leave home. I think they call it agoraphobia. I was too scared of the outside. Which meant, I couldn't take you to school, or anywhere, for that matter. So I had to take care of my mental health, and that meant leaving the country. Leaving you, which hurt the most. And which is why I want you here. I just can't go back there."

Jack munches on the tips of his fingers. "I miss you, too," he says finally. Then he waits a beat. "What would you and Dad do if I decided to stay?"

Another sigh, as loud as his dad's earlier. "Yaacob, there's nothing we can do to stop you. But trust me when I tell you—family is the most important thing in the world. You can chase the clouds, but eventually, they'll melt into the sky, leaving you lost. Anyway, I know it's late. But I'll call you again tomorrow. Make sure you eat enough; your face is too skinny now. Don't forget how much I love you."

"Love you, too, Mom."

The call ends, and Jack's back to the text message screen, which has the unsent:

I don't want to leave

He stops. His fingers hovering over the keyboard. And then his gaze leaves his phone's screen, and he looks all around, before finally settling on the poster of a flying Iron Man taped to his wall.

120

Next to another poster of Percy Jackson, staring out at the dark sea. A smile fills his face . . . but is gone in an instant, suddenly wiped away from his memory.

Then he deletes the message altogether, and sends:

I'll talk to you tomorrow

That was it.

I knew he didn't want to leave, but why couldn't he have told me that?

"Well, now you know," Time says. They turn to me. "Why does your face make it seem like this jaunt of ours has just made your decision a lot harder than it's supposed to be?"

How do I tell them that they're right?

CHAPTER TWENTY-ONE

Back in the Chronosphere, a curiosity tugs at me.

Iron Man and Percy Jackson. The posters in Jack's room. Oh God, he did not—how could he have remembered? Because that's just so cheesy.

But, since we're already in the Chronosphere . . .

"May I?" I ask, pointing a finger at the windows around us.

Time nods. "It's not as if you'll cause any more problems than you have already. The Chronosphere is quite sturdy."

I flick at the windows, until I see a cluster of me and Jack. Then I go through those, until I see exactly that day. All the way back then.

It was the first day of middle school and there I am, Past-Me, reading a book on the bench by myself at break, which was my favorite thing to do.

And there he is. On the swing. That kid. The one with the fauxhawk.

I'd never seen him before.

But there Past-Me goes, flipping pages of one of his favorites, which he'd read like five times already.

As that other kid swings higher and higher and higher to the point where even Past-Me can't stop himself from staring at him.

I remember thinking how brave he was. Seriously, after less than a minute on it, the boy's almost parallel to the ground.

And just when he's close to doing a complete revolution, he leaps off and lands ten feet away with a perfect dismount, on his haunches real low, doing a pretty perfect Marvel superhero pose, with both fists balled up.

Then he looks up, stares at Past-Me, and runs over all excited. "Did you see that? Tell me you saw that. That was the most perfect landing I've ever made. Did I look like Iron Man?" he asks.

But Past-Me's face is super transparent. He obviously thinks this kid is a joke. "You think you're a superhero? Just because you did that?"

The kid's shoulders slump in an instant, all wind knocked out of him. "Damn, dude. Way to kill my vibe."

"I didn't get a good look, anyway. I'm reading." Past-Me expects that to end the conversation.

But instead the kid asks, "What you reading?"

"Percy Jackson."

"Oh. See, you like superheroes too."

It takes Past-Me a second of wondering if there's some common ground to be had. "Percy Jackson isn't a superhero. He's a demigod."

"Same difference. They both have special powers and try to save the world. I love the sci-fi ones and you love the fantasy ones."

"Huh, I guess that's kinda true."

"I'm Yaacob, but I go by Jack."

"I'm Hazeem. And I go by Hazeem."

"Not Haz?"

Past-Me makes a face, as if he's just tasted something awful. "Why would I go by Haz?"

"Because I'm guaranteed to save at least twenty seconds every day, since I'll be saying your name a lot. Y'know, since we're best friends now."

"We are? When did I agree to that?"

"Right now. Iron Man and Percy Jackson. Together."

Past-Me actually rolls his eyes. "You're weird. But I guess we can be weird together."

And that was how Jack and Hazeem started.

He used to come over to our house all the time. My parents would treat him like he was my brother. Which got kind of odd, because my feelings for him shifted into something more as the years passed. I knew, of course, what those feelings meant. And I wasn't ashamed of them. But still, Jack meant so much to me, and I couldn't risk losing him. I promised myself I would never tell him how I felt, even though I knew I would always always always have a special place for him in my heart.

But then I broke my promise to myself in one stupid, drunken moment.

My body pangs with the remembrance of all that I've lost. I just hope Jack eventually understands that I am not his enemy.

That someone who feels this way about him can never do anything bad to him.

That one day he will understand I only want the best for him and if giving away my life to him was the only way for him to keep living, then I don't regret it one bit.

CHAPTER TWENTY-TWO

By the look on your face, it's obvious," Time says, hands in their pockets.

I probably don't have to ask. "What do you mean? My face is not an open book."

"No, it very much is. Your eyebrows tell the best stories, we swear. But we thinks that wet head meat of yours is deciding on not taking Jack's years back."

So guilty. And so wordless. "Okay, so my face is a wide-open book."

"Yup. Those caterpillars over your eyes, we're telling ya. Gotta shave them off or something," Time says.

But as we exit the cluster of me and Jack, I'm distracted by a pool of darkness from a floating window a hundred yards away.

"What is that, and why does it look so different from everything else in here?"

Time glances over, grins with menace. "Oh, that's you."

"What do you mean? How am I sucking all the light out of here?"

"Don't you want to go check it out?" Time says, leading the way, adding a silly glance over their shoulder.

And so I follow along, and we come to a vision of me, in bed, right after Jack had texted me that night after the fight. But my room looks . . . off. The light from my desk lamp looks dim, as if something in the air is interfering with it. "Why does it look like I'm in a black hole or something?"

Time shakes their head, points a finger at Past-Me. "There . . . you see the dusting? Those are time molecules."

I look closer and swear I see the air and light moving ever so slightly. "I remember you mentioning it. But wait a sec . . . what's with the sparking?"

True enough, the dust that's sucking in every photon of light then seems to spark, on and off, like fireflies. I mean, they're coming to life, almost as if energized, while Past-Me lies there like a frozen burrito.

"Now that is when the molecules mutate. Apparently, you were so embroiled in your emotions, and being so stagnant in your movements, that the time molecules sat around doing nothing as well, and they got so bored they practically burst out of their seams, and started detaching your years."

Mary Shelley seems to be hopping off the bubble dome, excited as she is. *Why does it look like radioactive Dorito dust flying around? Great. Now, I've got the munchies.*

"That's a good way to put it." I continue watching the microscopic dust, which suddenly becomes a new fascination. How could I have done this? What exactly are time molecules, and how exactly did I become a fusion reactor for them, to cause this major influence, something that's never happened in the history of time, according to Time? "Who knew doing nothing could be so . . . miraculous and devastating at the same time? My slothiness actually led to something!"

"In this case, nothingness seemed to be a virtue." Time watches with wide eyes, really studying the frozen figure to make sure Past-Me's mistake won't ever be repeated.

There was a lot of me lying around this past year. Just staring at the ceiling, staring at Mary Shelley, wishing something would happen. Even having to go to school was such a pain. I would just go through the motions, but the moment I got home, I'd go back to doing more of the same. I wouldn't even bother reading or doomscrolling on my phone. I would just do nothing and breathe. It was almost as if I had to force myself to calm down. And the more I did it, the calmer I felt, and the less I felt, too.

The less I felt. Which is kinda true, the more I think about it. It's like, every day that passes would leach my emotions away from me. Leaving behind whatever nothingness would leave behind.

Basically a giant, cavernous, empty space.

And so went the story of how I kept discarding parts of myself, which reminds me of an actual tale that goes kind of like that—something about the statue of a prince, and . . . I struggle to remember the rest.

"Well, it looks like it did indeed help for this phenomenon to have occurred," Time says.

I look at them with a question mark on my face.

They continue. "Your friend's life got extended, didn't it? The boy named Jack can go on living as if you had never existed," Time says. "Speaking of, how many actual moving time minutes have we spent on this one kid friend of yours? Feels like we've been dwelling and mulling and moping around for centuries."

"It's only been a microsecond. Frozen in time, remember?"

Time's back to their merry self. "And look where it got you! Traveling with yours truly. The incomparable Time."

Watching them, something occurs to me. "It's almost as if you wanted this."

"What? To have the entire timeline on the brink of collapse? We can assure you that is not something we would want."

"No," I say. "A travel buddy. A friend."

Time is stunned into sudden silence, their face a serving platter of emptiness.

So I take my opportunity, because I've just remembered the story that popped into my mind a minute ago. "I remember reading about 'The Happy Prince.' It was this really valuable statue of this guy on a pedestal who was all smiley, and he was covered in gold and rubies and all. But he was sad, so he convinced a sparrow—that was flying south for the winter—to find out how the people in his city were doing."

"Are you saying we're the prince or the sparrow?" Time asks.

"Doesn't matter. They were just together, you see. Anyway, the prince heard that there were people suffering all across town, so he decided to peel off the gold and dig out the gemstones and donate every valuable part of his body to each one. Asking the sparrow to take up the task, until the once shiny, colorful golden statue no longer was."

Time seems to contemplate every angle of the tale. "We don't know stories. Although is that it? The sparrow and the statue lived together happily ever after as a couple? But how would they mate since he was of the motionless kind?"

"Uh, no. They weren't lovers. They kind of ended up together, but not in a good way. It was too cold for the sparrow to keep going, so it lay at the statue's feet, too tired, and eventually died there."

"Ah. Touché."

But then I start thinking about myself, and the Happy Prince. I wasn't trying to do that, was I? I wasn't trying to give parts of myself to make sure others would live happy lives while I died at someone's feet—because that's just a little nauseating.

"Why're you cringing like that, to yourself?" Time asks, suddenly taking a step back. "Do we need to make a swift exit, because it seems like you may be conducting a funeral for your sanity?"

Even Mary Shelley looks at me with concern.

I can only shake my head. "It's nothing. Just a weird thought crossing through my mind." Yet I can't help but think about what my end will be like, if I can't figure out how to fix this mess. Am I going to be taken as worthless by townspeople, and then melted down into scrap? "Do you think there's a way to take this power away from me?"

"Let's see," Time says as they scrutinize me from top to bottom. "Your power is absolutely gone, because you've given away all your loose molecules, plus some that the timeline had created willy-nilly because you chose to give an excess amount to your nana, which then put you into time debt. Don't even think of trying to produce any more time molecules, by the way. Because we don't want things to go into further disarray, especially with everything already looking quite grim."

Okay, maybe a question they won't see coming. "Do you think you would like to be either the Happy Prince or the sparrow one day?" I ask.

But they're unfazed, waving it away as if it's an annoying gnat. "Us? Time? Be like one of your stories? Oh, don't be ridiculous. We have too many important things to take care of. You are all an immeasurable speck in the timeline. Seriously. Fourteen billion years and humanpeoples and your stories have subsisted for less than nothing. If we were to take all the grains of sand on the planet to account for all of time, then your existence is not even the tiniest neutrino in a speck of sand. Now do you understand how important our mission is? This is billions of times bigger than you and your not-very-friendly friend. But clearly you've made your choice with him."

Now that Time says it that way, an incomprehensible weight drags my shoulders down.

Do I really have to do this?

Time's rolling their eyes. "Not that it matters, but we would be neither the prince nor the sparrow. We would be the pedestal, propping up all of this entire existence. Anyway. Bored is us. On to the next."

And with a snap of their fingers . . .

CHAPTER TWENTY-THREE

Time's ripped me from one past into another.

This time, to deal with the history of the shadow who lives across the street.

Holly.

"We think it's time. As much time as there can be to waste. So, let's keep zipping through until all of this is resolved, yes?" Time says.

Ugh. Fine. I hold on tight to Mary Shelley, my only constant for this entire trip.

She looks up at me. *You can do this. You know her. She knows you. I actually still do like her, if that's any help?*

We're in the rundown house I've known for years. The one that quickly became friendly when the two kids who lived across from each other became fast friends.

Time's snapped us into the living room, with the hardwood floors and the flat-screen hung on the wall above the fireplace. It's the absolute opposite of our living room—this one feels super homey, as if it's made for anyone and everyone to just "Stop on by for some fresh lemonade and an oatmeal raisin cookie! Just come on in—the door's unlocked!"

Music from the early aughts pipes down from upstairs, along with a jarringly bad yowling trying to mimic the actual singer.

And there's the shadow, now in person form. On the armchair.

Holly's just a couple of months younger than me, with the brightest blond hair and the biggest blue eyes. But there's something about her, specifically her energy.

She's restless, hardly able to sit still. Her hands seem to be everywhere but attached to her own arms. "Can we just do something, like, I don't know. I just want to help get things off your mind," she says.

This was almost three months after my dad died and over a month since the Jack incident.

Past-Me sits cross-legged on the floor, super focused on his phone. "I don't know. I'm not really in the mood for things nowadays."

They're both obviously immune to the terrible singing from Holly's mom upstairs, white noise after years of suffering.

"I know, I know. And I don't want to always badger you about stuff. But like, maybe we can just go outside. You're looking a little too vampirish for my liking. Besides, the sun gives you vitamin D, which I hear is super useful for making bones and stuff."

"Do I need new bones? You're saying I can't just slug my way through the rest of—" Past-Me simply shrugs and mumbles, "Whatever. Let's do it."

Holly leaps off the couch and disappears through the kitchen, while Past-Me heaves himself off the floor and follows suit.

Time snaps their fingers, and we're now outside with the duo.

Holly hops around, while sipping on a blue Gatorade. "Tell me how I can get you out of this funk."

But Past-Me simply stands off to a corner of the backyard. "Holly, my dad just died. I don't think I'll be getting over it soon."

"Sorry, that's not what I meant," she says, sounding genuinely apologetic and a little embarrassed. "I don't want you to forget that. But I also want you to realize that we've got a whole life ahead of us. And just because Jack stopped talking to you doesn't mean you won't have another boy talking to you soon enough."

Past-Me lets out a rueful laugh. "Yeah, right."

"There are so many other cuties in Burbank. Hell, this is LA. This is where Hollywood stars are made. All the movies, TV shows. Lots of hot boys out here."

Past-Me cringes at thinking about being with any other boy. "Um, I don't know if I'm ready to date an actor. I'd rather eat a chainsaw. While it's running."

"You're right. Why did I even say that? Actors are the worst. My mom used to be a theater nerd, and she'd complain about how actors had to be 'on' and 'performey' all damn day. Must be exhausting to have been her. Always having to wear an emotion and put it on full display."

There's no doubt that Holly wants only happiness for Past-Me, and she thinks a distraction like "other boys" can help him get through his troubles.

Oh, she didn't really know me at all, did she? But maybe it was my fault. Maybe I didn't quite trust her enough to let her in on how I actually felt about Jack?

She really wanted me to be happy, but I think it had something to do with the fact that her mom was always so controlling of her life that maybe she needed to help me with mine instead?

And even right then, Past-Me looks up at the bedroom window and sees Mrs. Rainier watching them in the backyard. She unlocks her window, then yells out, "All right, Holly. Time for your shower and then dinner. Hazeem, you can come over again tomorrow, if you'd like. But only for an hour, because Holly's got lots of studying to do with me."

She's never been able to let go of her daughter. Her baby girl.

And sometimes, I wonder who was actually at fault for what happened to Holly.

CHAPTER TWENTY-FOUR

What in the heck was that?" Time asks, as we exit back out to the Chronosphere.

"Uh, that was Holly. The one you wanted to see next," I say. "Why? What were you expecting?"

"But nothing happened. It was the most useless intro ever. Not even worthy of a narrator."

Even Mary Shelley seems to nod.

"Oh my God, you two are killing me." What the hell am I going to give them? I mean, I guess we can always move on to the serious stuff. "Fine, you want something? Get ready for Storytime. So, Holly has always reminded me of Ariel, from *The Little Mermaid*, who grew up under the sea, always wishing to be part of someone else's world. Part of the prince's world because she didn't like the life she was stuck with."

Mary Shelley and Time are both focused on me with large, unblinking eyes.

Now I've got them. "Holly was homeschooled, and her mom wasn't big on letting her do any other kinds of activities that might allow her to meet other people. The only reason we got to hang out was because we lived so close to each other."

Time raises their hand. "But what did the young girl like about you? Your long-windedness? Or your inability to ever make a decision. Ever?"

I give them a glare so loud, they actually zip their lips shut.

So I continue. "This is also why Holly saw everyday things as super exciting, like going out for a walk all the way to the grocery store. That simple act brought her so much life. It was both sweet and a little sad that something so small felt like 'living on the edge' and 'a life truly worth living.'"

It's funny how if you've been caged your entire life, the tiniest taste of freedom could be the sweetest. Past-Me never needed to try and widen her mind in any way, because Holly is just so naturally curious. Mrs. Rainier would be by her daughter's side all day long, seeing how she worked remotely from home, and as a single mother with no one else to take care of her daughter. Her mom had never stopped her from getting a cell phone, though. Holly had every type of social media. Apparently, that was okay, as long as her interactions were monitored. All these wild thoughts invading her mind, as long as there were no wild people getting near her in person.

"But around this time, it was all starting to come crashing down in her young brain. Holly was getting restless, and her mom's grip seemed to get even tighter," I say.

In the Chronosphere, I flick through the windows, until we get

137

to the day that changed everything between us. "I need to show you how I ended up giving her those twenty-two years."

We step through a door covered with ivy, and end up on this one day, a month later, when she'd dragged Past-Me all the way to the garage.

Holly has a wondrous stare at her mom's Range Rover and decides, "Hazeem, it's finally time."

Past-Me's on his phone, but looks up briefly. "Time for?"

"See, my mom's on her work call, so she's super distracted. And I've been watching all these how-tos about driving."

Past-Me's instantly on high alert. "What're you planning?"

"I think I'm running away."

"What?" It's as if all time has stopped. "Where?"

"Disneyland."

Past-Me's laugh is uproarious. "That's forty miles. Not quite the definition of running away."

"Look, my mom will never take me, because she doesn't believe in 'monetized and manufactured happiness,' as she puts it, but I want to find out for myself." Holly grabs a stepladder and climbs up to the rafters, then pulls down a suitcase. "I've got all my essentials in here. Fruit Roll-Ups. Jar of peanut butter. Band-Aids. I want to check it out on my own."

"But, Holly, you can't do that," Past-Me says, finally realizing the seriousness of what's happening that second. "You don't even have a driver's license."

"I learned it all on TikTok. So, you wanna come with?"

Past-Me stares into Holly's eyes, and what he sees there is a wildness he's never seen before. And also a determination, a brightly burning flame that can't be easily doused. Not with any commonsense negotiation. "Holly, let's talk about this. You can't just leave."

She isn't entirely surprised by the note in his voice. "I'm going with or without you. At least, come with me to Union Station, and I'll drop you off there, and you can take the Metro home?"

I can only shake my head as I watch these two little clueless kids—fine, I'm only months older than them—try to discuss something so ridiculous.

Past-Me is torn. "I can't. Your mom will hate me forever."

"Fine." Holly unlocks the car, tosses the suitcase in the trunk, then climbs into the driver's seat. Then with a twist of the keys in the ignition, she starts it up. And with a quick jab of the garage door button, which she'd seen her mom press a million times, she's almost out.

Past-Me begs her to stop, yanks on the driver's side door.

But Holly merely locks it.

Then she's off, with the poor boy chasing after her.

"I can't believe she did that, as misguided as it was," I say to Time. "And all I could do was try. I didn't stop her. I only tried to. Without realizing how bad things were going to end up."

"We can't comprehend," Time says, even as they watch this scene with curiosity. They snap their fingers, and we're suddenly at the intersection on the corner of our street. The one that meets the main road. "But we are certainly invested."

For a moment, everything seems fine. Holly steers perfectly. And comes to a perfect stop at the crossroads. But she's got no clue that other drivers are usually the problem.

So before Past-Me can catch up with her, she hits the accelerator—

And a pickup runs through the intersection at forty or more, ignoring the stop sign—

Holly gets so flustered, she spins the steering wheel and slams on the gas instead of the brakes, as the SUV goes faster and faster, missing the offending vehicle by mere inches and instead screeching onto the sidewalk going no less than fifty, aiming straight for a giant oak at the opposite corner—

Seconds later, metal kisses wood with the loudest crash, and a giant plume of smoke climbs into the sky—

Past-Me screams and runs toward the previously familiar vehicle, now with a crumpled hood. He finally catches up, panting and winded, his voice hoarse as he calls Holly's name. When he gets to her side, she lies in the driver's seat, unmoving.

Her head—and the cracked windshield—are bloody.

And all Time can do is snap their fingers.

CHAPTER TWENTY-FIVE

We're in the hospital, the same hospital in Burbank I was born in. But this time, I find myself in the trauma wing.

Which is where Holly had been taken.

Past-Me's with Mrs. Rainier—who has been silent the entire time we've been here—in the waiting room, when the doctor, an East Asian lady, finally appears.

She's solemn as she updates them on Holly's condition. "She's stable, but unfortunately we're not seeing any brain activity," she says.

Past-Me sits there in shock as the doctor tosses around words like "brain dead" and "no quality of life," ending with a sad but definitive "a decision will need to be made."

All for a joyride and hope for a life of her own.

Mrs. Rainier floats away, through the hallway, practically a

ghost. She doesn't even have the energy to tell Past-Me not to follow, so he drags along behind, even with the doctor's odd side-eye,
yet she doesn't stop the young boy from tailing them.

Time, me, and Mrs. Rainier simply follow along. A quiet
procession.

They finally make it to the room where Holly is being monitored, countless wires and cables attached to her head, but despite
them, the brain wave scanner shows no movement.

Holly's mom perches herself at the edge of the bed, then threads
her fingers tight through her daughter's. Seconds later, her body is
racked with sobs.

"There was nothing to say. It was all too much," I croak out.

The doctor makes her exit, again giving Past-Me an odd look.
As if he doesn't belong there.

All the boy can do is sit back in the rigid plastic chair and stare
at the wall because he can't believe he's just lost another friend.
This time, seemingly forever.

I remember all the thoughts that went through my head then.
Like, if I'd just gotten in the car with Holly, if I'd offered to drive
instead, if I'd screamed for Mrs. Rainier, if I'd stopped looking at
my phone for a text from Jack for more than two seconds, if I'd
done so many things differently . . . maybe I could have saved her.

It was as if the space in my heart was being emptied out further.

Then I see it. The fog in Past-Me's eyes clearing away, and
he perks up. He—we—saved someone when all seemed lost once
before. Maybe we could do it again.

Time catches on, too. "Ah, we thinks you're about to say those
not-quite-magic words."

So Past-Me does the only thing he can do. This time, he says it under his breath, but with a determination. "Holly, you have to live. You have to." He pauses, then adds, "Twenty-two years."

And just like that, the brain wave machine goes berserk, the oscillations becoming these intense figure eights that dramatize all the newly found brain activity, as it goes *squawk* and *screek*.

Mrs. Rainier bolts up. "What's going on?"

A nurse runs in and stares in disbelief as she checks the scanner for any malfunctions. Just as quickly as she appears, she dashes out of the room again.

Then the same doctor reappears. And gasps.

Because Holly's eyes are open.

They stare at everything. Everyone. With a mixture of wonder and fear and elation in them.

That was the magic number three. Three for Past-Me, thus reinforcing his belief that he was fully capable of granting anyone life, if they truly needed it.

Something in my old self was convinced that maybe, just maybe, if I gifted everyone with those additional years, that they'd be grateful for having more time to realize their dreams, to spend time with family, to travel the world, to just live.

But looking back, I wonder if I would have taken the additional twenty-two years if someone had wanted to give them to me? I'm not sure, to be honest—and it feels like I'm the only one who wouldn't know.

If someone's life is full of empty, how can additional time fill all that void?

Mrs. Rainier is sobbing again, but this time with happiness. Holly looks at her like she's from a different planet, but still offers a scratchy, "Where am I?"

But when Past-Me approaches her, face beaming, her eyebrows bunch and she says, "Who are you?"

Past-Me's face falls, the words not quite sinking in.

Even Mrs. Rainier steps in and offers, "That's your friend, Hazeem, sweetie. Don't you recognize him?"

And the elation in the room leaks away when it becomes clear she doesn't.

The doctor finally advises Past-Me to step out—he shouldn't have been in here in the first place; it's for family only.

I look down at Mary Shelley. "Yeah, it's hard to suddenly be excluded."

Mary Shelley merely yawns. *Tell me about it. I'm a hamster. I'm always excluded as I continue to stay in a ridiculous bubble backpack. Why're you looking at me like that? It's either this or the royal palace you've built me.*

"And so, we can go this way, or that way, but anyway . . . ," Time says.

They snap their fingers, and it's just after an hour of Past-Me sitting alone in the waiting room, when Mrs. Rainier finally appears.

Her eyes brim with tears, swollen from everything. "Hazeem, what are you still doing here?" she asks. There's usually an edge to her voice when she speaks to me, but she must be too tired to muster it.

Past-Me stands and only answers, "How is she?"

Now, I can see how she weighs her options. Thankfully, she chooses to share. "It's a miracle, really, that she got out of the coma. She's still awake and talking, but the accident severely damaged her brain. They still need to run a bunch of tests to see the extent of it all, but her memory . . . well, she can't remember much. She's very confused and so, so scared."

Past-Me can't believe what he's hearing. Holly is in so much pain. He didn't want to lose another friend, but it seems like he may already have.

"Well, this is no fun," Time says. "Let's just skip, shall we?"

"Wait, we can't just—"

A snap of their fingers. A week later, and Past-Me sits by his desk, gazing out the window every five seconds, when he sees Mrs. Rainier's new wheelchair-equipped minivan pulling into their driveway. And in the passenger side, Holly—with her head wrapped in bandages. Past-Me hovers by the window, unsure what to do.

But minutes later, he sprints out of his room, down the stairs, and out of his house.

Mrs. Rainier's the one to open the door, a curt expression on her face, and Holly is visible behind her, in the living room, in her new wheelchair.

"Hazeem, now is not the best time. We just got home—"

"Please, Mrs. Rainier," he begs. "I just want to say hello."

Holly's voice comes out from behind her mother, "I think I know you."

Both Mrs. Rainier and Past-Me look at her in surprise, as the older lady rushes to her daughter's side, "You remember Hazeem, honey? What do you remember about him?"

"I'm not sure . . ." Holly stares at Past-Me a moment as if trying to place him. Then her face changes, contorts into confusion. "It's all a little hazy . . ."

Past-Me feels the need to try. "Holly, we're friends—"

But Holly just gets more upset and agitated because she can't remember. Mrs. Rainier stands and rushes Past-Me out the door before he can get another word in. She blocks him from Holly's view and tries to let the boy down easy. "We appreciate you coming by, Hazeem. But Holly needs time to heal. She has a long road ahead of her, and I think it might be best if you let us handle it in private."

She sounds tired. So, so tired.

Past-Me knows not to argue. "I'm sorry" is all he can muster.

As Mrs. Rainier swings the door shut, Holly gives Past-Me one last look.

"She got hurt because I was too busy to pay attention to her, truly listen to her. Why should I even try to unstick time if people are going to keep getting hurt because of me?" I ask.

Time only shakes their head. "We don't know what it's like to be one of you, so we have no advice to give. Other than to fix the timeline, which is the number one priority for either of us."

There's a pause. An awkward one. Hanging between me and Time. Which I can't feel bothered enough to address.

They tap on their chin. "But you are forgetting one more person."

Ah, yes. One more twist of the sharp knife to my gut. "Yeah, I know."

"Precisely. Before we move on to them, does this mean that you are not willing to take those years back from Holly?"

I don't know if she's happy or not. It's not that I think her injuries are holding her back—Holly can do anything she sets her mind to, regardless of any kind of circumstances—but all she wanted was freedom, independence. And now her mother has more control than ever, has more fear of losing her than ever. Maybe that will change once Holly has had more time to recover and adapt to her new normal.

But the future is so uncertain. Ugh. "I don't know what to do. This is impossible."

CHAPTER TWENTY-SIX

I have a question about this Holly person. What befuddles me is how she'd been given everything in life and still was unsatisfied. She got to go to school at home and hardly had to leave her house. She got taken care of by her mom and she had a friend—you. That would be everything, wouldn't it?" Time asks.

We're back in the cemetery, but in the parking lot this time, leaning against my Mini. I just had to get out of the Chronosphere after that whole ordeal. Some fresh oxygen, plus all the green around me was pretty much needed.

It's still amazing how, as bright as the sun blazes away on this August afternoon, I don't feel a degree of heat on my skin. "There's more to life than just staying at home and doing nothing. I mean, there's *life*, and there's *living*. You're granted a life, but what you do with it is the living part."

Oops. This is the moment I realize I'm obviously talking out of my ass, considering the nothingness that my life has become since my dad died. Because I'm pretty much running on an empty tank of cares, without any way to fill it back up.

How unlucky of Jack and Holly to have a friend like me. It's almost as if my time molecules are contagious, and I'm not just handing out life but spreading death as well.

"Holly wanted more," I say. "She wanted to see the world. She wanted to be out *there*. She wanted to be her own person, not under the charge of her mom until the day either one of them dies. When Holly's dad left, her mom started to overcompensate. She was extra attentive, extra protective. And that turned into being extra controlling."

"You're sounding more and more worked up. Are you thinking too hard? Is that what's happening?" Time asks.

I shake my head. Thinking doesn't hurt. It's the realizing that does.

Time paces the length of the car, then all around it, before hopping onto the trunk and lounging on it with a squeak of their orange overalls. "And yet, the three of you have found problems of your own. You, especially. You reek of utter discontent."

"That's not fair. And besides, you don't know my life."

"But we do. We know everything in your timeline. We know everything about your mom. We know everything about your dad. We know your mother barely talks to you. About anything at all. Especially *him*."

It somehow stings even more to hear someone else say what's true. "Yeah, well. That doesn't mean you know me at all. That's just the basics."

149

"Incorrect. Time knows all," they say with a casual flourish and a bowing of the head.

"So you know what it's like, then? To be me, a human?"

"We sure do because—" Time's tongue seems to have frozen. As frozen as everything is around us.

Aha. I've successfully stumped them. Yay, Hazeem. A thousand million billion gazillion points for this one victory against the being that controls one major part of everyone's existence. "Yes? You were saying?"

"You know what? With the way you keep crowing about it, we don't think we would ever have the want to be human. You all seem to be utterly fixated on every single incomprehensible minutia. It seems like all of you live by a code, and that code is 'drama.' Because, you know, things could be a lot easier, but you'll choose to focus on one tiny detail instead of looking at the big picture, as we have to. In fact, need we remind you that we've documented thirteen point eight billion years of past existence, plus an indescribable number of years that have yet to happen, which can still happen, if you make up your mind already. Do you want time to end? Do you want to know what you're potentially erasing with your indecisiveness?"

Yikes. That's a whole lot of complaining. "Uh, no?"

"No, you don't. Because it's not just your present timeline. But other multiverses as well. The split ones. We take care of those, too."

"Yeah, I don't need to know about those."

Time purses their lips. "It'll make you feel really, really, really, really, really bad. Trust us. Are we telling the truth? Or are we not?"

"You're confusing me."

"Sounds like the perfect time to make your decision, then!" Time says.

Now I see what they're getting at. Even with all the time in the world and beyond, they're getting impatient. Trying to trick me. Well, I have some tricks up my sleeve, too. "I want to show you what it's like to be us."

They raise an eyebrow. "Us, as in human?"

"Yes. I want to take you somewhere."

"We really don't have the—"

"Time? Now, we both know that's not true."

CHAPTER TWENTY-SEVEN

We're back at my middle school—the very same one I went to with Jack—and we're about to swing.

Literally. We're staring at the swings in the playground.

"So . . . you've brought us here to . . ." Time says, pointing at the rubber seats.

"Just get on it," I say. "And hold on."

Time first takes a seat, then turns to look at me. "Okay, now what?"

I give them a push, and they move forward a foot.

Then Time simply falls face down onto the rubber flooring. They hop to their feet, and say, "That was very brief. How was that supposed to be enjoyable at all?"

I groan-laugh. "I told you—you're supposed to hold on to the chains!"

Even Mary Shelley looks like she's chuckling.

So we give it another try, with them gripping onto the metal links hard and tight.

And then they take off. Back and forth a few times. Until they come to a stop. Not understanding how to pump their legs, they don't get the right momentum going. And when they do try that the first time, their legs flail in each and every direction.

"Stop with your giggles! This isn't exactly intuitive," Time yells at me.

But I can't help clutching my side from laughing so hard.

And there it is again. The foreign sound from my throat.

I have missed it.

We give it one more go, with a more detailed explanation of what they have to do to make this work.

They finally get the hang of it, and when I see them climbing higher and higher, I get onto the swing next to them.

For a few minutes, here we are. Just letting the wind rush through our ears.

I have missed this.

All I can think of is how much easier life would be if I could just get on a swing every damn day. There's just something about it—even as life tries to rush all around me, the simple act of going back and forth, back and forth, brings so much stillness to my mind.

Because, when I get on a swing, all my troubles seem to melt away.

Even now, some part of me feels a tiny tickle somewhere in my gut, and I can't explain what it is, or how it's happening. It seemed to happen earlier when Time made me laugh. It feels familiar, but I can't quite place it.

"What's this whooshing thing reverberating through us?" Time asks, stopping their swing with a kick-up of dust.

"That's the sound of wind."

"No. We know about wind. Do you feel a tiny tickle somewhere here?" Time says, pointing to their gut.

Whoa. Not even sure how to broach that subject. And why we're both experiencing the exact same thing. "Maybe it's a bit of gas? Maybe all the wind went through your nose and down into your belly and . . ." I don't even know where to go with this.

Time pokes their stomach. "Yet we don't feel anything now."

Yeah, I don't feel anything either. Is that a bad thing, though? "Well, you're not swinging anymore. So, how was it?"

"How was what? Also, why did we have to do this swinging thing?" Time asks.

"I thought it could've been fun to show you something . . . fun," I say, realizing just how long it's been since I did anything I used to enjoy. I've forgotten all the things that I used to do that really made me feel good.

Time squints an eye. "Why're you making us do these things? We're proud to never do anything ever. We don't even walk amongst you."

Just the smugness on their face says it all.

Pretty sure they're lying. "Are you telling me, and I'm asking this in the nicest way possible, that you've never walked with people?"

They shake their head. "We've been busy, you see. Because time is a very busy construct, and there are no holidays to be taken from them."

"So you've never hung out with any of us? At least, before me?"

They shake their head again.

"Never had any food? Watched a movie? Listened to music?" I ask.

The face they make is one of obvious displeasure, as if they've just sucked on a cranberry. "We've probably heard moo-sic at some point. But just in case, describe it to us."

"It's . . . an arrangement of melodies?"

Time merely shrugs. "Sounds meaningless."

"Sounds can have meaning."

"Why does it seem like we're trapped in a mind maze of your making?"

An idea forms in my mind. "Can you take me somewhere else?"

"Where would you like to go?"

"Anywhere it's raining."

"Odd request." Time looks at me, then spins in place, a finger pointing out, before stopping dead in their tracks. "That way."

They snap their fingers.

We're in a forest. And while everything's frozen, I merely have to glance over at Time, and they snap their fingers again.

And the rain pours down on and around us.

Why are you trying to get us all wet? Mary Shelley seems to say, as she covers her head with her paws.

I don't remember the last time I played in the rain. But here I am. I think "frolicking" is the right word. And there's that tickle in my tummy again. And the wetter I get, the wider my smile seems to be, until my cheeks start to ache. "Do you hear that?"

Time's orange jumpsuit has transformed into a neon-orange raincoat. "We thought this would be auspicious for the occasion. What did you just say?"

"Do you hear the rain?"

They look up at the sky and get pelted with a couple splashes of blobby raindrops. "It's hitting our face more than our listening organs."

"Just listen."

Time focuses, stares at the ground, then at me. "There's a rhythm."

"Right? There's a rhythm to everything, I think. And sometimes, I just have to listen, and it's a melody I've heard before."

Time listens intently. "Rain. And is that also wind we hear? It's quite an orchestra."

"I figured you'd be more attuned to this than Ariana or Mozart."

"Are those types of cheeses? We hear they can be quite a treat for humankind."

My face is now pure marble, with an immovable expression. "Yes. Cheese. Because we're talking about music."

Time seems to be listening intently, while staring at the greenery around us. Their pupils dilate as they cock their head to one side, almost as if they're understanding something they've never tried to comprehend before.

Then they tap their forehead. "We have been acquiring random data into our knowledge stores. But why does it feel like you're merely delaying things? There's one more person we've yet to see."

And they snap their fingers.

CHAPTER TWENTY-EIGHT

Back in the Chronosphere, and we've stepped through a doorway made out of bamboo.

We're a few paces behind Past-Me, who's skulking through a park, who's keeping himself at a safe distance from Yamany, who's making a giant loop around the Burbank Library, before heading to the back of the building and hiding behind a row of hedges.

"I guess we're going right in, huh?" I say, recognizing this moment immediately. "No buildup whatsoever."

"Figured it's best to just get going with it all already," Time says. "Why are we walking so slow?"

They're back in their orange jumpsuit, and we're still taking our time, with Past-Me trying to avoid being noticed.

Oh, you've told me of this one, Mary Shelley seems to say. *By the way, I'm on your side through all of this.*

Yamany's twisting the hem of their flowery romper, with their phone glued to their ear, sounding quite upset as they stare at the hedges.

By the timbre and tone and wail of their words, this is obviously a call of crisis. "I just don't know if I can do this anymore."

They pull a fountain pen from their pocket and do finger gymnastics with it, twirling it around and around, floating it on their knuckles, all in a very fidgety act.

It is a one-sided conversation, but Past-Me seems to know what's being said on the other end, as they hide behind the corner wall. His breathing's getting heavier and heavier, as he weighs his options about what's going to happen.

I'd been friends with Yamany for almost a year now, and while we weren't super close, they'd opened up about some of their struggles—they were happy in their identity, but others weren't, and it definitely took a toll on them. I just didn't know how big that toll was.

Yamany shakes their head. "No, I'm at a park."

Past-Me simply watches, not having a clue about how to handle this situation.

Yamany continues on the phone. "I just . . . yeah, I have it in my hand. It's one of those old-fashioned fountain ones with a sharp metal nib," Yamany says, staring at the pen with an intensity that should scare anyone.

Silence. And a sudden rack of sobs overcomes them.

"No, I don't want to set it aside. I don't want to get rid of it, or throw it away. No, I think . . . I think I'm . . . I think I'm going to do it right now."

Yamany says that with a grave finality in their voice.

I watch Past-Me tear apart at the seams, both of us wondering what's the right decision to make. Past-Me's head swivels around—this way and that—and a worthlessness settles into his bones, because at that age, who would have trained you for such an incident?

Yamany's still on the phone, seemingly getting more frustrated than before at the inevitable being delayed, as the pen casually conducts a silent symphony in the air.

Both Past-Me and I feel a fatigue settle in. And that fatigue cloaks a ton of hopelessness in it.

Past-Me could've called the police. But Yamany and I are both brown. And if the police thought they had a weapon, something that could hurt others, who's to say we wouldn't be facing the muzzle of an actual weapon turned on us.

Past-Me could've called out, stepped in, stopped the whole thing from happening, but there'd be no way to stop Yamany from attempting once again. But that didn't mean he couldn't try to help them right now.

Time watches alongside, their face etched with a level of curiosity I've yet to see on them. "So much turmoil in one person. Very confounding, and utterly head-boggling."

Wow. That's the first thing I've ever heard them say that comes close to identifying with one of us. I even give Mary Shelley a quick glance.

Yup. I heard it too. You weren't the only one.

"They were going through so much. I barely knew the half of it," I say.

"Yes, it's a wonder sometimes when humanthings are unwilling to trust others in confidence. Because how much easier would it be to traverse the landscape of frustration you all seem to be mucked up in," Time says.

We watch as Yamany holds the pen aloft, removes the cap, and is two seconds away from plunging the very sharp, fine-point nib into their wrist—

When Past-Me does the only thing he can think to do, as he whispers to himself, "I need you to *stay* for the next twenty-two years."

The pen fumbles out of Yamany's fingers and tips backward, splotching out a burst of ink that plops everywhere over their romper.

And at the very moment, as Yamany is awestruck by the patches of blue on their body, they are suddenly distracted by the formation of a pattern on the fabric.

They stare, hypnotized, by the swirls that form almost as if by magic, because nothing else, not chance or coincidence or luck, could have produced it.

Never in a million years could a single word be written out in such randomness:

stay

"Very *Charlotte's Web* of the universe, huh?" I say.

Time doesn't quite get the reference.

Yamany ends the call quickly with a finger-punch of the red button.

Past-Me knows something has changed. And he lets out a huge sigh.

Which instantly gets Yamany's attention. "Who's there?" they blurt out.

Past-Me's face is a tangle of horror and fear. He could've run away, but nah. Instead, he makes himself known to his friend. "Hey, oh my God. What're you doing here hiding by the bushes?" he asks, sounding like a bad actor.

Yamany simply looks at him, wondering if it's a coincidence. They stare down at the word imprinted on their romper, then up at Hazeem. "What're *you* doing here? Were you following me?" they ask.

"No! I was just walking around trying to clear my thoughts, and just bumped into you back here. Cool romper, cool design. 'Stay' is a very powerful word. Did you just buy that? Wow, did that pen just explode? Maybe you should, like, just throw it away or something."

It just wasn't the coolest of distractions.

For a brief moment, Yamany seems relieved, their mind off what had happened. But a second later, doubt creeps onto their face. "Why do you want me to get rid of the pen? Were you listening in on my conversation?"

Past-Me's mouth is a giant black hole. "What conversa—okay, I didn't mean to, I just . . . I'm worried. I followed you from the library. Listen, if there's anything you want to talk about—"

Yamany quickly gathers their things. "I don't appreciate being eavesdropped on. None of this is *any* of your business."

I reach for their arm. "Yamany, please—"

But they wrench it away. "Stay the hell away from me!"

And then they storm off.

I had put an end to the friendship, at lightning speed.

CHAPTER TWENTY-NINE

Wait, wait, wait. Let me guess. You want to show us what Yamany went through to get them where they're at right now," Time says.

Am I that predictable? I mean, I only want to explore a tiny bit of what my friends were like, if I have to make the damn decision about which one has to lose their life. Instead of saying that, I say something a little nicer. "I don't think there's any way for us to fully understand how Yamany ended up where they were, but maybe we can try."

Time fluffs the pants of their orange jumpsuit with their hands in the pockets. "Sure. Let's do this, as if we're not rushing for time."

In the Chronosphere, we go peering through Yamany's windows, until we find one of them having dinner with their mom and dad. In this one, they've got a healthy, lush beard and long hair down to their shoulders. They're dressed in a tight pink sleeveless top and a long, black skirt. What's most pronounced is that giant smile they have on their face as they giggle about something to their parents.

It's clear they are having the best time as a trio.

This Latino family is at a Mexican restaurant, and they are happily sipping on drinks and dipping chips in guac.

It's obvious their parents love their child very much. Their mom even reaches over and grabs their hand, "I'm just so proud of you for being who you are, Yamany. You've never looked happier."

Their dad lays his hand on top of the pair, and says, "Just remember, you are your own person. And don't let anyone take that away from you."

"Oh my God, you're both embarrassing me with how cool you're being." Yamany blushes, turns away to look out at the crowd across the street, then notices a middle-age white woman staring at them.

She's with a child full of smiles—presumably her daughter—who's waving at Yamany. Until the mom sneers while whispering something into the girl's ear.

The expression on the woman is of disgust, and it clearly sends Yamany into a spin.

Their dad takes a look at the woman and girl and instantly turns back to his own child. "Hey. It's just us. Family. We're the only ones that matter. I want you to understand that you can come talk to us about anything, any day. I know it can be hard, but just know that we're on your side. You have to live your most authentic self."

Their parents grab each other's hands and squeeze tight. It almost looks as if they're in a prayer circle, except that they have chips and salsa before them.

It dawns on me that this is what healthy parenting looks like.

Taking care of your child's needs, protecting and supporting them, loving them unconditionally. Everything they're doing is the right thing, and it's nice to see there are still good people in the world.

I had this with Dad. Mom, too, before she lost him.

But would I ever make a good dad? Especially when I have no clue if I can even make it through adulthood unscathed, since I'm already a severely wounded animal, yelping on the roadside, seeking help from anyone passing by?

But Yamany takes it all in, instantly transported back to their original level of brightness.

Their mom takes a sip of her frozen margarita. "You know, being nonbinary in this world is still a new thing to a lot of people, and I don't have any problem with educating anyone. A lot of people see the world in black and white. So what if you're a little bit grayer than they're used to?"

Yamany twists the hem of their top. "Well, I'm glad you're both so positive. This would've been a lot harder without you two."

Their dad has a tear in his eye. "You are the best child we could have ever wished for. And I'm just glad that you're gonna grow up to be an amazing human."

"Whenever you're ready to talk colleges, just let me know," their mom says. "Even though I know you love working at the library."

"Yeah, books are kind of my world," Yamany says.

A pang of something regretful pongs my insides, because it's amazing to see my wonderful friend be showered with so much love, even if they experience meanness at times.

The waitress brings out their entrees and as they chew on their burrito, Yamany pauses for a second, staring out into the distance, as if suddenly unable to taste anything anymore.

Time watches quietly, then says, "Maybe it's just our view of your entire world, but it certainly looks as if they're wondering if all of this is worth it."

CHAPTER THIRTY

There were other incidents after that, when people did more than just stare, when the hurt wasn't just on the inside. It's hard being queer in this country, or in this world, actually. And people are still being attacked for it.

Yamany and I connected over that shared bond, but I didn't experience the level of hate they did on a near daily basis. I only wish I could have told them that I will fiercely and ferociously protect them as much as I can, if given the chance.

Back in the Chronosphere, Time flutters their lashes. "So that was your final option. What now?"

My time's run out. They want an answer. A decision. "After all this you really think one of them deserves to have their life taken away?"

"Well, it's not about what anyone deserves. It's about what you have to decide."

I have to keep trying. "What if I show you what life was like for the four of us before everything fell apart? Show you why I care so much? Show you the good times?"

Time rolls their eyes. "So what good times are we talking about? Because all we've seen is dysfunction and abandonment."

I think long and hard, until my brain starts to ache. Because the good times seem to fade away when you're deeply mired in the not-so-good.

I sprint from window to window to window in the Chronosphere, through thousands of them, until I find a moment of me and Jack at the skateboard park.

And off we go through the door.

It was more than a year ago when he'd decided to take me there.

Well, I'd always gone with him. But this day was a little different.

There he is, talking to Past-Me, as dozens of other skateboarders fly around us. "Hey, come on. It's time for you to finally try."

"Uh, no. I'll stick to my very safe book, thank you," I say, perched on the bench at the outer edge of the park. "I'm not going to ever get on that flying, skull-shattering piece of cardboard, you know this. With everyone zooming around us and all the jostling and banging into each other, I'm good."

"Come on, Haz. Just once. I promise I will take care of you," Jack says with clear pleading in his eyes.

And somehow even a good memory is made painful, knowing that was no longer true.

Mary Shelley's bored, yawning away. *You two again? Come on already. Give me some good ol' action.*

Time's by my side, hypnotized by all the activity, then clapping hard when someone does a flip on their skateboard. "Why does that look like a whole load of excitement?"

"What do you mean, you'll take care of me?" Past-Me asks.

"Grab my hands," Jack says, as he holds out his palms.

Past-Me can only stare at them. "They're so smooth, mine will just slide right out of them."

"Fine. I'll hold on to your hips, so you won't fall. How does that sound?"

"But that's still pretty dangerous, isn't it?"

"Nah, I promise you'll be fine. Seriously. Then you'll see how fun it can be. And you know that's what I'm here for."

And so, for the first time in his life, Past-Me puts his book down, heaves himself off the bench, and walks over with really shaky legs. He places one foot onto the gliding board and instantly loses his balance.

"God, how embarrassing," I say.

Past-Me almost gives up.

But Jack grabs onto his hips. "Come on, let's do this again. Try one more time."

That one simple gesture sends a shockwave of confidence in Past-Me. And because it's hard to say no to Jack at this point, Past-Me gets back on the board. One foot first.

Jack slowly inches his hands away, but instantly grabs a hold of his hips again. "Hold on tight to my shoulders. Come on."

"It's almost embarrassing to see how happy I was to be with him," I say.

God, it's so obvious, my feelings for him. How very quickly I got so deeply entrenched at that time.

No one gave any mind to us two boys.

And eventually, after tens of tries, Past-Me finds his balance, even if he's still very wobbly. But if Jack hadn't been there, he would've fallen flat on his face and broken his nose or his wrist. But no, Jack holds on fast to him.

To me.

And he says he will never let go.

God. I don't know how long I can hold on to that.

Because he did eventually let me go. And all I've been since then is a ship that's lost its sails, anchor, and rudder, letting the ocean winds drag me out, to everywhere.

Jack continues to guide Past-Me, as they glide forward, inch by inch, until finally after ten feet of moving, and making their way back to the bench, Past-Me hops off and says, "Okay, I've had enough. I think that's good for now."

Time remarks in a sultry whisper, "So you two had quite the bond, obviously."

Ew. Definitely makes me a little uncomfortable. "We had a lot of fun."

We exit the scene and move from window to window in the Chronosphere, watching the progression of Jack and Past-Me visiting the skate park every day. And how Jack taught me more and more.

Until a month later, when Past-Me glides along on his own. Without any of Jack's help. But the smile on the latter is so bright, realizing how his efforts have paid off.

"Who'd have thought little nerdy me could ever be on a

skateboard!" Past-Me says, making Jack laugh. "This is probably the bro-est thing I could ever do."

Jack's so proud of his best friend being able to do the one thing he loves most. Because now, they can do it together.

And then when Past-Me makes a whole round around the park, Jack gives him an actual standing ovation, saying, "Wow, looks like I'm gonna have to save up and get you a skateboard of your own."

And Past-Me couldn't have been happier, as he says, "I want one with blue wheels."

CHAPTER THIRTY-ONE

Back in the Chronosphere, my mind's still caught in a whirlwind of endorphins at seeing that part of my history, but thrown into the whole chaos is also the realization that I'll never have that again.

I can't help but stare at all the windows and doors around me, wondering if there's one in the future that'll take me anywhere close to it again. What's yet to happen can always change, can't it? But that's also a question I fear to ask, because what if every configuration of the future fails to ever get me and Jack together again?

Even though I did look happy and content as Future-Me, hanging out on the sailboat with that guy. The one with the scar that looked like a 7 on his palm.

But why do I even hope that Jack will ever want to talk to me anyway? He must think I'm the biggest jerk there is, to have taken advantage of his kindness.

God, how I wish I hadn't had a drop to drink that last night of ours. Then things could've been totally fine. He wouldn't have fallen off the edge of the roof. And we'd still be skateboarding together.

"There's that eyebrowy face again," Time says, fluffing the pants of their orange jumpsuit. "They're starting to look like squirmy worms trying to mate with each other."

"What?" And I make one that looks like I'm beyond consti-pated, as if I'm straining to even get a thought out. "You mean this face?"

"No, this one." Time sticks their teeth out and flares their nose, so they kinda look like a donkey.

"You're not trying to make me laugh." But a chuckle escapes my throat.

"Oh, why do you think we are?" This time, they put on doe eyes and switch to duck-pouting while making *gloop-gloop* noises with their lips. "We're only trying to show you what you look like when you look all emotional. Not sure why you think it's attractive."

"Will you stop?" Yet I can't help grinning. "I do not look like a drowning goldfish when I'm deep in thought."

"When was the last time you looked in the mirror?" Time asks with a side-eye.

I can't help but smack them on the arm. "Can you focus? We need to see Holly now."

Time raises their hands as if in surrender, then reconfigures the Chronosphere.

And we're browsing through moments between me and Holly. Specifically, the happymaking events.

But there's one important moment that surpasses them all.

"There's this one time, when we were at the mall. This one right here," I say.

Seconds later, Time and I are trailing behind Past-Me and Holly.

Holly, who's always been super sheltered, who rarely gets to even step out of her own home by herself, gets this one special hall pass for a Saturday, all because I had given my word to Mrs. Rainier. And also because her mom had to have some people over to work on stuff at the house, and she didn't want them anywhere near her daughter.

Holly was practically bouncing off the walls, staring and pointing at every single thing. It's almost as if she's never gone shopping before—really, she's just never been without her mother.

And I'd never been to the mall with a friend like her, so getting to see it for the first time through her eyes was quite an event.

"Anything you want to do?" Past-Me asks.

Holly's head is like that toy on a car's dashboard, the one with the springy head. "I don't know. I want a lemonade. Or maybe a cupcake. Or maybe a soft pretzel."

So they go get an Auntie Anne's pretzel, and a Sprinkles cupcake, and then a lemonade, before they walk around the mall.

Even Time's a little astounded. "This girl . . . was she on portobellos?"

"What? Why would she be on . . . Oh, mushrooms? Why would you know a thing like that? Also, I think you're on the wrong track there, buddy," I say, with a roll of my eyes.

Time merely shrugs.

Mary Shelley's chittering too. *She was definitely on something. No one's that hyperactive. Not even me when no one's around.*

173

After rounding the mall twice, Holly's making her way to the food court.

"You hungry again?" Past-Me asks.

"So many things I want to eat," Holly says as she twirls her long, blond braid.

To the food court they go, to get a slice of pizza each.

And as they grab a table to figure out what to do next, Holly calms herself down and says, "You know I have ADHD, right? But I don't know if that explains everything about me?"

Past-Me merely nods as he sips on a Diet Coke. "Yeah, I know, but it makes sense especially now, watching you gawk at everything around us. Your attention span is kind of nonexistent."

Holly makes a face as if she's just chewed on a fly, not liking the flavor. "Ew. Thanks. But I agree. My mind's just going on overdrive, being so overloaded by everything. Like my brain is going a million miles a minute. And I'm like, staring at this, looking at that, and my attention's just all over the place."

"How do you handle all of that?" Past-Me asks. "Like, what helps the most?"

Holly winks, then leans in, about to share the dirtiest secret her innocent mind knows. "Meditation. I know, such a disappointment to be such an oldie. Can you believe it? Me? See, sometimes when things with my mom get a bit too much, when she's a bit too controlling and too intense, I lock myself in my room. And I sit on the floor. And I just clear my mind."

This blows Past-Me's mind. "Whoa. But how? Doesn't meditating require extreme focus? Don't you still get distracted?"

"Nah, not like that. At first, I thought that was what meditating was. That it was like swatting away a million mosquitoes—where

174

each thought is a buzzing bug—which ended up not working. So I thought of something that moves but can also be still, if that makes sense? Which led me to go with the flame of a candle. So I just think of the flame flickering every now and then because of wind or somebody walking by or a light breeze, and I make it go still. And I realized that maybe the correct analogy is that the flame is my mind, and the flickering is every single thought trying to invade my brain. And then I just remind myself that it's almost impossible to have a steady flame all the time. So every time a thought tries to invade my brain, something that tries to take me away from my meditating, I just focus back on trying to still it. Plus, there's nothing quite like the darkness being brought to light by a candle. You should try it sometime."

"I don't know if I could do all that," Past-Me says.

"It's simple! Let's just sit here. Close your eyes and think of a candle like I said and then clear your mind and focus on the burning yellow and orange and sometimes blue."

I can't help but snicker as I watch the two with their eyes shut, in the middle of the chaos that is a mall's food court. "Yup, there's me, trying to think of a flame, and then suddenly imagining a cheeseburger. Then some Popeye's. Then homework. So many things trying to distract me from, oh God, everything. I remember focusing so hard on the flame that I got a little stressed out. And that's only after thirty seconds."

Time's at a nearby table, eavesdropping on two boys checking out a game on their Switch. "These two sound as smart as cardboard. Sorry, were you saying something crucial to our journey through time?"

I simply wave them away. "Carry on and do whatever you want."

175

But in truth, I remember how all the noise around me started to drown out and then it was just me and the flame. Plus, a certain measure of calm and peace I hadn't known in a while.

"And then when you're ready," Holly says, "just open your eyes. And that's it."

Past-Me opens his eyes and sees the world unchanged, and just shrugs.

Maybe it will become useful someday. But for that moment, he simply smiles back, as if everything in the world is totally okay.

CHAPTER THIRTY-TWO

Time's busy scratching their head as we exit back out to the Chronosphere. "These pasts of yours seem a little . . . what's that word for when you're missing your elbows and knees?"

"What? I don't think there is a word for that," I say.

Time scoffs. "Of course there is. Ah! Disjointed? 'Twas at the tip of our tongue. But truly, your history has been all over the place. Now, where is this happy thing you keep talking about?"

"Happy isn't a thing. It's a feeling," I say.

"Ugh, not one of those feeling things again," Time says, with all the drama of a bad stage actress. "Right, Mary Shelley?"

But the hamster is already asleep in her bubble dome backpack. Poor thing must be exhausted from staying up this entire time.

Which kinda reminds me . . .

"Quick, I want to check out this one time Yamany took me to the theater," I say.

Time's already got the windows and doors and stairs reconfigured. "Say when."

I browse through a bunch until I find the one I'm looking for.

Time peers through the door's window, at a poster. "What is a *Matilda*?" Time asks.

"It's this book by Roald Dahl, an author who loved telling some very wicked stories, and it was adapted into a musical. But it's not us watching the musical that matters. It's what happens after."

So we find the moment of us at the library a month later.

There they are, an excited Yamany, saying, "So, after we watched *Matilda*, I thought of this idea for an author workshop. I pitched it to our head librarian and she loved it! We invited a local author and they're going to lead it. They've written some young adult novels, and they're going to do a quick intro class on writing. I'm so excited—I'm helping run some of it, but I'm also going to be taking the class. You should join!"

And so it was that day that Yamany convinced Past-Me to take his first writing class. The pair learned how to generate ideas and how to not be obsessed with finding the right words as they crafted their prose, and about revising and sometimes finding those perfect words later. After three exhausting hours, everyone had written their very own one-page short story, something very few of us had done before.

"Hazeem, you should be a writer. There is a glimmer in your eye I've never seen before!" Yamany teases Past-Me after the workshop.

"Yet we don't see any such bright light coming from you," Time says, also teasing but in a more jabby way.

"I had fun," Past-Me says, surprised at the truth of his own writing.

But now I see the glimmer Yamany was talking about. I don't know if I want to be a writer—I feel like you don't have to be a writer to want to write. It is a good way to talk about all your feelings, though.

And maybe that's just it.

Everything in the stories we read is infused with the author's experiences, kind of like the short stories that we wrote that day.

"What did you write about?" Yamany asks.

Past-Me stares at the page full of scribbled words. "About someone searching for a missing memory."

"Oh, that's interesting. Why would they do that?"

"Because they only have an hour left to live, and they can't remember the name of their favorite teacher from first grade. So they take a journey into their brain, to uncover this memory."

"Whoa. A little dark, but also super intriguing in a funny way," Yamany says. "I wrote about a clam that wants to become a supermodel and so they borrow a pearl from their oyster friend. It's kind of like coming out of your shell and facing the world. But with the help of people you love."

"That sounds adorable!"

"I think it is. Kinda proud of myself," they say, with the brightest blushing of their cheeks.

"Maybe you're the one who should be a writer. It seems like your brain operates in an entirely different dimension," Past-Me says.

Yamany looks even prouder at those words. "Maybe? I don't know. I feel like embracing my true self has helped me to see the world through a different lens. I finally feel like I can say and do exactly what I want. Maybe it's something you should consider doing."

"What? Me? I'm the most boring person I know," Past-Me says with the weirdest chuckle.

"Maybe there's something, or *someone*, out there you're interested in expressing yourself to. Maybe writing to him can help."

It's Past-Me's turn to blush a deep red. "What are you talking about? There's no one."

Yamany simply rolls their eyes. "Hazeem, I know you've got a thing for Jack. You can't stop talking about him. It's about time you consider telling him the truth."

"But . . . I don't think I'm ready to risk our friendship."

"Okay, okay, I get that," Yamany says, thankfully letting the subject drop. "But if he's your best friend, and I'm your best friend, and Holly's also your best friend, why have we never hung out together before?"

Past-Me chuckles. "I don't know. I guess I like things the way they are?"

"Life has to change eventually. It took a while for me to accept who I am. And then once I did, I transformatized and became the best version of me that I ever could be. Don't close yourself off to that."

"What are you trying to say? What is it about myself that I should change?" Past-Me looks utterly confused.

"No, no, no—I'm not saying you should. I'm saying maybe one day you'll look at everything around you, and you'll finally tell yourself, this is it. I'm good. I'm happy. There's nothing else I would want."

I still think about that moment. I was so afraid of change even then, and with everything that's happened in the past year, it's no wonder I couldn't handle it.

As if I'm deserving of any amount of happy.

CHAPTER THIRTY-THREE

Time has snapped us back to the house, to the living room. They're hovering by the credenza, just staring at me. With an exclamation point above their head.

"Why are you looking at me as if I am about to do something drastic?" I ask.

"It's not as if you're about to do something drastic. It's as if you're about to do much of nothing. Imagine a pit, and we dig a hole to make it even more holey. That's what you are. Full of nothing. A bottomless pit."

"I don't think that means what you want it to mean."

But they're right. I'm very much full of nothing. Just absolutely frothing with it. And nothing is exactly what I've been doing for the past year.

"Why do you look like that? I thought those were the happy moments and happy was good," Time says.

"It is. Those were moments where I was really happy. But seeing them now . . . it's just hard to see everything I'm missing out on. Everything I've lost."

"What do you mean? Explain."

"My friends taught me so many amazing things. Holly taught me to find stillness in myself. Yamany taught me how I should express myself. And Jack taught me to not be so afraid of everything. But it's like I've forgotten all of that. It's like I'm nothing now. Like I'm numb. And that's actually the scariest thing—that I don't . . . I don't care about anything anymore."

"We have no clue what this numb thing is," Time says, with a blank look on their face.

Oh God. More explainy stuff. "It's the lack of feeling, like you're not afraid of anything, or you're not frightened or . . . I have no clue how to properly say this. It's as if your inside's a vacuum and all it does is suck in everything everyone's giving you, except there's no giving back. All that empty space is eating up everything that you know, even all of reality, and maybe even time."

Because it's true. All those days of me moping around in bed was a huge timesuck, and I'll never get those precious hours back.

Time takes a seat on the couch. An orange ship in a sea of white. "We'd like to hear more of it."

"Let's just say that after I lost my dad, maybe I also lost my interest in everything. Which is why I've turtled, and it's made me not care much about anything anymore."

"Oh, is that a good thing?" Time asks, scratching their chin.

"Maybe not caring for anything means you're not afraid of the timeline imploding."

But that's just it. I want to care. But why is it so difficult?

Time continues. "Listen. We are the caretaker of time, and that means we will do everything in our power to make sure that nothing about it goes awry, and that it returns to its original state. Do you understand?"

"You seem mad. Even though you've said many times you don't do emotions."

"We don't. What we do is time manipulation, time travel, time everything and anything. Do you want us to take you through a history of time, show you all of it? Well, maybe we should just take you on a journey through the future or a multiverse of what could happen if you decide not to do anything about this whole situation we're in?"

How do I tell them that we're going to be stuck in this situation a bit longer than expected?

"Oh, don't you dare give us that look," Time says. "We feel like we've been patient long enough, haven't we?"

"Yeah, but I also think that I should have a chance to figure out what's best for me."

"That's a very human trait, isn't it?"

"What is?"

"Selfishness. That's what humans are. It's all about that one person, yourself, or that someone you supposedly love, but forget about everyone else. And that's why we will remain as Time and we will never, ever want to be one of you."

"That's not fair."

"There is no fair!" Time yells. "It just sounds like you have no clue what you are. Who you are. What you want. Who you want. Nothing. Who even are you?" Time asks. "Maybe it's time for you to deal with it. Deal with yourself. You don't think we haven't noticed there's something we've been avoiding so far? One person you refuse to even ask to see?"

It feels like a giant wrench is twisting the biggest nut in my stomach.

Time snaps their fingers . . .

And we're back inside the Chronosphere.

Doors, stairs, windows, all start whirring around us. "No, stop!" I plead.

"It's time you face this, Hazeem!" Time says, while juggling the glittery golden ball.

The doors start slowing to a stop, and I begin to catch glimpses of him through their windows.

My dad. Look at that one. Why does he look so happy, staring at me, playing video games, in our living room?

In a panic, before the doors finish revolving, I slap the Chronosphere out of Time's hand, sending it rolling off down a stairwell.

And suddenly, everything around us starts to spin.

CHAPTER THIRTY-FOUR

The petulant act sends us into an out-of-control spin, the time-line suddenly out of control and out of sync Whoa what are we looking at I say Why did you do that Time asks Oh if you only hadn't done that I'm so worried because suddenly we're thrust into a realm of dinosaurs like I'm face-to-face with a brontosaurus I need to stop the Chronosphere from spinning Oh that really is a brontosaurus isn't it Wow Am I actually in like the Paleozoic Era or something How do we tell you that the Chronosphere being out of whack can take us all the way back to what earthly scientists had labeled the Big Bang all the way to the beginning of time to the birth of time and even farther out into the futures we haven't even begun to contemplate yet Now where the heck is that damn Chronosphere we just saw it here somewhere must've rolled down an invisible staircase What you're saying is we can go all the way back to thirteen point eight billion years ago and forward another thirteen point eight billion years but how would I know the passage of time via the traversal of light-years Oh come on can we go at least get my mind off things Time is flustered because the timeline has never gone out of whack I can't believe this is happening anyway and they have to figure out a way to get everything into whack If only there is a way to show Why is the Chronosphere still spinning Hazeem the past and the future aren't always exciting Wow why is talking so weird in this thing It's like I can hardly understand what you're saying Yes because when the timeline is out of whack thisiswhathappens Which is when we suddenly find ourselves in the middle of the American Civil War Oh my God what are we doing here We have no explanation for what just happened You do understand I finally realize that I am being flung around in time and as I stare at a cavalry of riflemen I panic because I'm a Brown boy and I'm not meant to exist in this era Brown people cannot time travel it's dangerous for us Then I find different clones of myself existing simultaneously which I can't ever explain but it's like seeing myself branch off into many different varieties Oh you are experiencing the multiverse silly boy Is that it but why are they all mostly of me doing nothing Because you end up doing nothing in most branching timelines you truly are a dull boy Oh my God you're telling me I can't ever be interesting or undull Yes precisely because you refuse to step out of your comfortness I sure can I mean look at that one going to Paris all alone Well anyone can do that Ding ding ding you sure love doing things alone don't you maybe you're indeed meant to be alone and lonely How dare you I am alone but I'm not lonely But how the hell do we break out of this It is time for me to decide what to do and I finally fling myself down a set of stairs that has suddenly appeared and grab onto the Chronosphere and—stop it dead in its tracks.

CHAPTER THIRTY-FIVE

Well. That was that. I must have the biggest question mark tattooed on my face right now.

"Wow, I had not expected a whacked multiverse to be that dull. I thought there'd be more things happening, like the movies make it seem. Like, you know, in one timeline, I'd be a zombie and in another, I'd be a nine-headed Hydra or something like that, right?"

We're back in the house. And Time is quiet, merely looking at me as if my face is a jumbled assembly of croissants. In their silence they purse their lips, and there's a slight wrinkle at the edge of their eyes as if they're actually angry, which isn't possible, since they're devoid of emotions. "What are you talking about? Zombie? Hydra? What are those things? Why does that salivary slug in your face hole insist on making things up and . . . oh, are they part of a human's movie world thingie?"

"Ew. What did you just call my tongue? Wait. Are you actually furious at me?"

Even Mary Shelley is deathly quiet in her backpack. *You really shouldn't have done that. That magic golden ball was their baby.*

But this accusation seems to shake Time's core, sending them into a state of askewness. "Fury? Are you saying we're suddenly in possession of an emotion? That's just not possible, is it?"

Their intense gaze leaves my face and skates away, toward everything around us, even out the living room window.

It's weird that no matter how we exit the past or the future or the multiverse, we end up in or near familiar surroundings.

"We have been busy taking care of everything. Making sure nothing implodes while you humanpeoplebeings have just been doing the dullest thing—even duller than the multiverse . . . that is, living your lives," Time says, clearly not done ranting.

"What else are we supposed to do? We have to do something with our existence. With our time."

Time cringes. "While we stand by to make sure nothing goes wrong! Although we have failed on this day."

That's kinda sad. Time shouldn't just have to wait around for something bad to happen, letting the world and life pass them by. They should be allowed to experience some of what we do.

"I've taken you on some exciting journeyettes of our own. You got to swing. You got to hear the rain. Don't you think you should be allowed to keep it up? Get to find out what other things the universe has to offer you?" I ask.

Time taps their chin. "Well, if we could have a feeling right now, it would be exasperated because you have duly exasperated us. We have been beyond nice. Now, we have the right mind to just leave you here as punishment. You know what? We'll do just that."

"Wait, what are you going to—"

I don't even get a chance to finish my sentence.

Because just like that, Time disappears.

CHAPTER THIRTY-SIX

Time is gone. Just blinked out of existence.

And I have no clue where they went.

And I'm just staring all around me in the living room, not knowing what to do.

And I slink away up the stairs, to my bedroom, staring out the window at all the quietness and frozenness in the world from up there.

And I do the only thing I know: I climb right back into bed, hoping that I can outlive all this nonsense. With Mary Shelley in her bubble dome backpack next to me. Already napping.

And I stare at the ceiling.

And eventually I drift off to sleep.

✦ ✦ ✦

I wake up, and it's just me again, Mary Shelley in her dome backpack next to me.

So I should do something.

So I climb out of bed and take a trip down the stairs.

So I think maybe Time was right. Maybe I need to start figuring out who I am. Maybe first I need to figure out who I was.

So I haven't grieved enough. Or maybe I haven't grieved properly.

So I make my way over to my dad's study at the far corner of the house, the quietest spot. I stand at the closed door for what feels like an hour.

✦ ✦ ✦

When I finally fling the door open, everything of his is still there untouched.

His drawing tablet, caked with dust.

The walls crowded with his many illustrations, all of them bright, cheery, and beautiful. Of animal best friends and children laughing together, everyone just getting along.

But on one section of wall, right in front of his desk, it's just illustrations of us, the family. Dad, Mom, Nana, and me.

And even though I'm in here, there's no life in this room.

But something else is missing, something I've always associated him with: the oftentimes nostril-scorching and vomit-deploying aftershave of his. With heavy doses of sandalwood and something super musky.

I'd always made a face at it, but I'd never been able to convince him to switch to a less pungent one. And so I'd gotten used to it, my nose stinging every time I'd step into this room.

But the smell that used to permeate every cubic inch of this room is gone.

That's when I start to wonder if maybe he truly has been wiped from every space in my life, that I've been living in denial, that someday, he'd come back.

A silly hope that the universe would return him to me.

The most ridiculous wish, I know.

But it's also the realization that, just like I've been letting everything go, I've almost fully let him go, too.

The mustache.

The smile.

The warm eyes that had nothing but admiration for me, his son.

Yet I'm still holding on to something. Something that randomly nags at the back of my brain.

Count not the years.

Do I even want to know what he meant by his dying words? I just can't. Not yet. Maybe not ever.

I take a seat at his desk and settle into the spongy cushion, as it takes all my weight. The same chair he would sit on as he contemplated how to work on the smile of a baby sloth as it had to go poop. Or an elephant as it had to mourn a dead friend. Or a kaiju who had to find a way to love himself.

And when things would go awry, he had no fear of erasing the entire project and starting from scratch. An entire blank, white, pristine window to what could be.

I'd sit in the corner when I was younger and go through heaps of picture books, some of them he had illustrated.

I would ask him how he would do the things he did. He'd say everything came with time and lots of practice.

And I think that's what I am not capable of—practice. Because I just haven't had enough motivation to get to any proficient level in anything I do. Why bother trying to do anything and everything at all?

Because, 'tis better when all is already lost.

I can't skateboard well enough. I can't even meditate because my mind is just so full of intense thoughts. And there's no way I'll ever become a writer.

Maybe I should start.

Okay, maybe I really should.

Can I, though?

Ugh, dammit. I've got to.

"Time? I'm ready for what's next," I say.

Nothing.

I call out again. And again. For a minute. Then another. Then an entire hour as I exit the house and roam the frozen Burbank streets, walking past everyday people trying to do everyday things, but failing to.

All because of me.

Where is Time? Don't tell me they were really . . . serious.

Suddenly I feel lost, not knowing what I should do next. Because I guess I finally got my wish of pushing everything away from me.

Now all that's left is all this space I have around me.

And maybe, all of time.

So should I get going?

CHAPTER THIRTY-SEVEN

I'm back at the house, still not knowing what I should do.

It's the weirdest kind of doomsday, for sure. Like, it's even hard to chew on the whole damn thing in my mind—that if the entire universe just stops moving, then that means everything is over anyway.

But maybe I should take advantage of whatever this stillness is. Maybe I should just get out there. Maybe I should practice being myself, learn what I'm capable of. Maybe I should learn to face my fears once again.

So many "maybes," yet only one "maybe" sounds the most feasible.

"Maybe" not.

I sit on the couch.

I take a nap.

I wake from my nap.

I play around with Mary Shelley. Let her run wild, but only as long as I can watch.

And then more nothing, for what feels like a whole day. I'm still by myself, alone.

There's a rough joke in there that I choose not to acknowledge, because even as the timeline is pending implosion I can't help but wonder if I'm the master of my own demise.

Maybe there's a way for me to figure this out without losing anyone.

How to gain some of the years back, repay some of the debt.

And so I pick up Mary Shelley and ask, "Want to go on a journey with me?"

She simply nods. Or she seems to. *I've been waiting for something exciting to happen in my entire hamstery life. Fine, there's this whole time conundrum, but since Time refuses to pay you any more mind, then let's just do our thing?*

We're in need of transportation if we're going anywhere. My car's back at the cemetery, so I head on over across the street, to Mrs. Rainier's and Holly's house. I go through the side gate and enter the back door. There's no one down here—they must be upstairs. Then into the garage. I don't think they'd mind.

A quick hop into their car . . . and the engine simply won't start.

Okay, so time being frozen means physics and chemistry can't simply work the way they're supposed to. I have to go old-school.

I run back into my garage and pull out my dad's dusty bike. *God, I wish I'd gone biking more with you.*

But I can't. I can't use his bike. It's his. I just am not ready to claim his possessions.

And then, out of the darkest corner of the garage, something peeks out at me.

A blue wheel.

My skateboard. Oh my God. It's there. Unused for months.

It's dusty, a little rusty, but the wheels still spin. Just a quick spray of WD40, and it's good to go again.

And with Mary Shelley in her backpack on my chest, I guess I'm ready to face the world.

Down the street I go, as I kick and glide. Kick and glide.

And this is it. It's me. Going God knows where.

Trying to kill time. (Oops, not literally.)

And maybe, just maybe, I'll find some new pieces of myself I can pick up along the way.

Now, where do I go?

CHAPTER THIRTY-EIGHT

I end up skateboarding my way out of Burbank, weaving through unmoving traffic on the 101, making my way downtown. No fatigue settling into my body—a benefit of time still being frozen, I'm guessing. So I keep going.

I explore what downtown has to offer. All the buildings around me. Places that I've lived so close to my entire life but hardly took the time to see.

And I keep going. Staying on the freeway.

Unsure which direction I'm heading, and because my phone's useless, how am I supposed to know how to get around, where to go? Until I remember my dad's mention of something called a physical map? That I can maybe find at a gas station?

So I stop by the nearest one and find one that's practically a textbook. I guess it'll serve me fine. Not even sure if I'll need it.

Although, maybe it'll help me if I get lost. Into the backpack it goes.

Then I stop by a Target to get a physical compass. At least now I'll have some sense of direction.

But where do I go?

Or, maybe, I should actually, really, truly . . . get lost?

I take the I-10 West, but it feels like it takes me half a day to even get to Santa Monica, to get to the Pacific Coast Highway.

I'm going north. And I can't deny the view along the coast. Just spectacular diamond-sparkly ocean against a sapphire sky.

I even catch a school of dolphins mid-jump. Huh. Fascinating.

Kick and glide. Kick and glide.

Mary Shelley stares and naps, stares and naps. We occasionally have a conversation, when she's interested in having one, but otherwise, it's just me.

Taking in everything around me.

With the sun not moving a single inch above me, it's impossible to know how much of the frozen present passes. Which I think is weird. Unless I'm the center of the universe, which, of course, doesn't make any sense.

Suddenly I'm staring at the Golden Gate Bridge.

Yes, San Francisco.

Time's just flown by.

I take this moment to walk around, staring at the people in the city and going up and down hills.

Wow. I've gone on a trip on my own. Something I would have never, ever attempted before. I can only imagine how Holly would feel in this moment. If only she could've joined me.

Maybe I can bring her here one day. Once I figure this time thing out, of course.

I try calling out to Time again, to see if they're listening. "I wish I could show you San Francisco. It's pretty nice here. Doesn't even feel cold, even though everyone's in a light jacket."

Silence.

So much nothing. And there's nothing else for me to do. Pretty sure I can't cross the ocean.

Do you really want to do that? Mary Shelley seems to ask, eyes all wide.

"I mean . . . why not try the impossible? Maybe we'll figure out something."

But before I do so, I stop by a bookstore, grab a few journals and pens, and throw them into my backpack. There's still plenty of space for Mary Shelley though; her dome is in the front compartment, all to her own, so she'll be fine. I want to document this. To always remember my first big act of doing something after a year of nothing.

I make my way to the ocean and select the nearest kayak I can see at the pier. But when I try to push it, it won't budge. The water is weirdly solid. I take a tentative step, and whoa . . .

I can walk on top of the waves. I can walk on water. Okay, insert godly joke here.

So I place my skateboard down and kick and go. And I'm actually going. I'm literally gliding across the surface of the ocean, over waves, just speeding along. And I keep going.

And I go and go and go . . . Until I reach a major group of islands, with the most spectacular, eye-popping scenery. Facing a stunning dawn, the sun splaying its rays everywhere.

Oh my God. How long have I been *going* for?

Is this Honolulu? Wow. I'm actually in Hawaii. And I get to see a place I've only dreamed of seeing. So many tourists around. Lots of people munching on breakfast.

Even though I'm not hungry—I haven't been since time had stopped—I grab a few bites of whatever I can see, while taking the time to write down and reflect on what I've seen so far. The volcano's pretty scary but kinda cool. I must've been there exploring for days. Maybe even weeks?

But who's keeping track?

And then I keep going.

I'm skateboarding along, in the middle of the ocean, in utter darkness. Well, not quite. There's an actual full moon, and it's enough to help guide me on my way.

When there's a sudden oddness to the frozen water. It seems almost as if it's in the middle of being whipped up into a frenzy.

Ah. I think I'm in the middle of a hurricane.

Okay, now I'm starting to panic, my breathing and heart rate accelerating. Because what if—

No, I can't think of that now. So I bring Holly to mind and force myself to meditate, as I stand here in the middle of the ocean, surrounded by mountains of water.

Even Mary Shelley seems to do the same, lying in her backpack with her eyes closed. Just breathing calmly.

And a few minutes later, I'm back to normal again. Gosh, it really does work.

Some of the waves are sky high, but I have no trouble skateboarding around them, up and down the salty hills, to avoid climbing their treacherous-looking steps. Who knows how high the fall is from the other side?

Of course, if Time decides to unfreeze everything at this very moment, things will get really awkward, and Mary Shelley and I will drown. But I document the moment in my notepad, and I keep going until I hit the calmness of the eye, with the bright moon peeking down at me—which is such a contrast to the bright sun of Los Angeles. But I don't overthink it. As we arrive at another group of islands in the Pacific Ocean.

I think it's the Philippines, just by checking out the boats and local architecture. Lots of fishermen trawling the waters in the dark of night. I hear they're an archipelago, with tens of thousands of islands.

Even though I'm terrible at art, unlike my dad, I briefly sketch out the scene in front of me, imagining children splashing around in the water. Just laughing away.

The journal's so full, I decide to leave it behind for someone to find. I stop by a local department store to grab some more notepads.

But I keep kicking and gliding, suddenly reminded of the strangest fact in all of moviedom:

That in the classic *Groundhog Day*—another movie my dad loved—the theory was that the main character was trapped in the repeating day for tens of thousands of years, evidenced by him being fluent in so many things—languages, playing the piano, his memorization of all the significant events of the day.

And by the end, he's a changed person. No longer the annoying, arrogant twit he started off as in the beginning.

Which then begs the question: How long am I going to be trapped in this frozen today for me to change who I am?

I can't even remember how many times I had to stop and just sit on whatever "floor" I could find, to seek stillness in my mind. Because being alone can wreak so much havoc up in the meat of my—as Time would call it—noggin nuggets.

Thank goodness for my constant companion, Mary Shelley. Conversations with her are keeping me sane.

Even if her random jabs about the pointlessness of all this are sometimes unasked for.

So I keep going. I guess Time will appear whenever they want to. I've lost track of how much I've traveled. And how much I've written and sketched out in notepads, which I leave at random places everywhere I've gone. Certainly this is not possible within an actual real lifetime.

How long have I actually been doing this?

I promise myself I'm going to try to see as many things as I can and taste as many foods as I can. And to document my feelings as I experience each one.

And through it all, the bright night light of this part of my journey stays in the sky, above me. Isn't it funny how, no matter where we go, no matter who we end up becoming, it's still the same moon staring down at us?

Mary Shelley and I end up in Singapore, then go on north to Kuala Lumpur and to Bangkok. I visit all the nearby landmarks—sometimes struggling to see them in the near-dark—and keep going all the way through to Shanghai, Kathmandu, and then Mumbai.

I make it to Istanbul and get to witness the beauty that is the

Ayasofya and the Blue Mosque across from each other. I find myself in Egypt, staring up at the pyramids, nestled against the night sky. And then through to Europe. So much amazing architecture in Rome—we don't have ancient buildings like this anywhere in the United States. And I make sure to stop in Paris, so I can see the Eiffel Tower.

I keep going all the way to the Atlantic Ocean. Am I actually doing this? It's utterly mind-boggling.

In the span of a microsecond, even though in real time it may be actual years, I have crossed the entire world, and now I've crossed a second ocean.

Then the sun starts to appear, as I head all the way down to Rio de Janeiro in Brazil, now in broad daylight, where I see the statue of Jesus with Sugarloaf Mountain in the background. Then west through the mountains of Chile. And up north, through Peru, Colombia, then all the way to Mexico, where I experience the ancient ruins of Chichen Itza.

After that, I cross the border to the country I grew up in.

Then a long and boring walk through Texas. Oh God. What a drag you are. Seriously.

And when I'm getting close to home . . . I wonder if it's finally time.

Time to find out who I am.

CHAPTER THIRTY-NINE

The house is just as I left it. Nothing's changed.

It's still just a house, though. Not a home. Hasn't been in a long while. And there's nothing I can do about it to make it—

Wait. Maybe there is something. Something that had so occupied me before I left.

I place Mary Shelley's backpack by her favorite spot at the window in the living room and dash to the garage. I grab the stepladder to get to the rafters, and there they are.

Boxes of Dad's belongings. This is where Mom had stored away her grief. She had to get everything that reminded her of him out of her sight. She never did explain why she did it so slowly but so intentionally.

I had to beg her to leave Dad's study untouched, instead keeping the door shut tight, and she honored my only wish.

Just need to find the one box, the only box that matters. And when I do find the one labeled "bathroom," I drag it down and gently place it on the ground.

I tear at the brown packing tape and lift the flaps open.

It's all of his bathroomy things. His electric toothbrush. His Dove men's body wash. His charcoal shampoo. Towel. Bathrobe. Trimmer. Shaving cream.

And the most important thing: the red-and-black gradient bottle of Fahrenheit aftershave. I pick it up with trembling hands.

As I pull off the cap, that familiar and overpowering whiff—I think it's sandalwood—hits me all the way to my insides.

I even subconsciously take a look around the garage, because it's almost as if my dad's right by my side, over my shoulder, just hiding behind the door to the house.

But no. He's not there.

I leave everything, not bothering to put the box away again, and make my way back into the house. The aftershave acts as a sort of diffuser, the smell evaporating and filling in the space around me.

Maybe if I say it out loud, something will be different.

"I miss him so much," I say out loud. "Time, do you hear me? I miss my dad."

+ ✦ ✦

I'm at the kitchen island, with Mary Shelley in her bubble backpack, the bottle of Fahrenheit between us.

She's wordless, like always. But this time she looks angry.

"Why are you mad at me?" I ask.

Because you choose to concentrate on the most inane things when you could be focusing on how to save everyone.

"Well, I don't know what to do. I'm clueless."

No, you're not. You know exactly what to do. You know exactly who to take the time away from. You're just scared to do it. You're just trying to find an excuse.

"I can't believe you're saying this to me, Mary Shelley."

I'm not saying this to you. This is your own brain talking to you.

I grab the backpack and the aftershave and make my way out into the living room, settling on the couch, so I can lean back and rest my weary head, heavy with a million thoughts. "I wish we could have some chocolate together. I think that'd be quite yummy."

I wish I could let Time taste it.

Listen to birds sing.

Play some board games.

Watch some Sandra Bullock movies, like the ones my dad loved so much.

"It's just us, isn't it? It's just us, as we try to figure out what's next. But how do I sacrifice the one person out of all of them?"

You know I'm also an option right now.

"I cannot let you go, Mary Shelley. You are going to die a twenty-four-year-old hamster."

What if I want to go? She's not looking angry anymore. Just sad, morose.

"Don't say that. You're my best friend."

No, I'm not. I'm just something you cry to.

"Don't you dare say that! You're everything to me, Mary Shelley."

I think you need to be institutionalized.

Anyway.

What if Time was here? What if Time demanded that you did

208

choose or they were going to do it for you? Me, or Nana, or Jack, or
Holly, or Yamany?

I don't have an answer for her.

It seems like you've been stuck in the present for what feels like
centuries. I feel like I've grown so many new whiskers simply having
gone on this journey with you.

"Yes, I feel different, too. But I think I'm done with this day,
Mary Shelley. How about you?"

Okay. Deep breath.

"Time. Where are you? I need to talk to you right now."

I cradle Mary Shelley in my hands because I need to feel some
comfort. "Time, I'm not kidding. Come back right now. I'm ready
to finish this. Or I swear I'll give my years away to some rando
again."

As if by magic, Time finally appears. With a smirky smile. And
a cabinet next to them, as they sort through a tray filled with iron
nails.

Ugh. I can't admit I'm not *not* happy to see them. But . . . "What
the hell are you doing?" I ask.

Time's busy putting away the contents of their tray. "Caught us
in the middle of filing our nails. We hear that's what humans do
when you get bored. Now, how does it feel to stay in this frozen
forever of today?"

I'm not going to let them win. "It wasn't too bad. I got to see
the entire world. Just wish I could actually remember what I tasted
along the way."

Time scrunches up their face and pouts. "Then why don't we
keep you here until time deteriorates to a point where it's no longer ever going to be rational."

"Ugh, why are you being so difficult?" A sudden despondency clouds over my entire head. "I feel like it's time."

Time interrupts with a tuneless whistle and waves the cabinet away, and it disappears. "We're literally right here."

"No, I mean it's time to make a decision. But I have a few conditions. First, you are right. I've been avoiding it for far too long. And I need to do this, so I can safely save the timeline."

"You are being very cryptic. It's not helpful at all."

I don't know how to say the words. They are kind of lost inside me because I've spent the entire past year avoiding them. Is it possible I'm following in my mom's footsteps of casual avoidance? "I just don't know if I can ever prepare myself to see my dad. I don't think I'll ever be truly ready to see him."

"Then now is the best time ever. This is your moment."

"I just don't know how I'll react."

Time cracks their knuckles, as if they know they have the answer to this perplexing question. "It sounds like he's had a huge bearing on your life. We think that's something worth investigating."

"I don't know if I can bear to see him leave me once again. There's just so much pressure to make this count. I feel like I should go in prepared."

"What do you mean?" Time asks, rounding their lips into an O to start whistling again.

"I feel like I should have a list of questions. Ask him all about his life. Or life in general. Advice. Practical things. Anything. Everything. And to ask him what he meant by his dying words."

"What dying words?"

"The same four words that I've never understood. 'Count not

the years.' I have a vague idea of what they could mean, but every time I get close to grasping it, it escapes me."

"You can only view your time with him. You can't change a thing. But maybe you can find clues in the day to figure that out right now."

Something inside me wants to believe in Time. That Time has the best motivation of all, better than mine. But somehow I doubt if they have the best of intentions.

"Why do you look like you're doubting us, Hazeem? Look, if you decide to not take back any of the years you've given away, then the only thing to do is . . . Well, let's not get to that just yet. So, what do you want to do?"

"Let's do it. Let me go back to the day. A year ago from today. The day my dad died."

CHAPTER FORTY

From the Chronosphere to here.

Back in my bedroom.

"Can you stay?" I ask.

Time appears confused. "Where else would we be?"

The alarm clock reads 6:44, then switches to 6:45, suddenly blaring out loud.

Past-Me hops out of bed, sticks a finger into Mary's tiny plexiglass house on the desk to tickle her head, then ambles to the bathroom for a shower.

"Aww, look at you," I say. "How brown was your fur back then?"

Mary Shelley, in her bubble dome backpack, looks totally uninterested now, staring at her younger self.

We then follow him down to the living room, where he sits,

playing a game on his TV. Waiting for the first dawning of life to appear in his house.

"I used to do this in the mornings on the weekends, especially when I was addicted to a game that just came out," I say, standing at the bottom of the stairs.

Until the footsteps.

There he is. Coming down the stairs, with a heavy stomping of tired feet and an intense rubbing of bleary eyes, while scratching at his lush mustache.

My heart. It's thumping so loud, the *whooshing* drowns out the sound in my ears.

It's him. My dad.

I get to see him again. But he has no clue I'm here, and my hand swims through nothing as he walks past me.

The aching that's nearly faded away from my chest this past year seems to pulse harder and harder, as if it's seeking vengeance at my forgetting.

Especially as that aftershave sears through my lungs.

"Hazeem, typical Saturday, huh?" Dad says.

"Yeah. Mom left already?" Past-Me asks.

"Thirty-six-hour rotation. She's not even been home yet."

They go about their separate ways in the house.

"I never meant to take him for granted," I say. "But I guess . . . it just happens."

Dad disappears into the study to do his work. Past-Me keeps playing his favorite role-playing game.

Time snaps us to hours later, when they reconvene for lunch. Heating up some Chinese leftovers, and munching away at the dining table. Both of them scrolling endlessly, silently, on their phones.

"Meeting any friends today?" Dad asks, while spooning a giant heap of General Tso's chicken with rice into his mouth.

"I dunno. Maybe Jack? I think he's free today."

Dad has an odd expression, something I've never noticed before.

When lunch is done, they go back to their usual.

"So is this what you beingthings call a 'relationship,'" Time says, watching the pair go their separate ways again. "Because maybe we can have a 'relationship' with anything, since it feels effortless. Seriously, there's barely any effort required in it."

I can only shrug. "You wouldn't understand."

Time snaps us to later that afternoon, when Dad finally crawls out of his cave with a sore back and a groaning stretch. "Let's go to Griffith? Been a while since we headed over there."

"No! Don't!" I say, even though I know I can't change the past.

"Sure," Past-Me says, finally turning off his game.

They drive over, chatting about nothing important. While Time and I sit in the back, just staring out the window the whole ride.

After finding a parking spot along the road, they stretch tight muscles to prep for the hike. It's steep at times, and very dusty, but they make it all the way up to Griffith Observatory after an intense and sweaty hour.

This was us. Super casual. Nothing demanding. Just . . . easy.

Past-Me yawns and says, "Let's check out the observatory. Been years since I stepped in there."

Dad simply bumps against Past-Me's shoulder. "My son's never been the scientific one."

214

"Yeah, but it's never too late for me to geek out."

Together, they enter the hushed hall of the observatory and wander through the exhibit. In the theater, they watch a short film about the mysteriousness of space.

But fifteen minutes into it, Dad starts to squirm and wince, as if uncomfortable in his own skin, before breaking out in a cold sweat. "Let's go, Hazeem."

"Why? The show's not over yet."

"I don't feel so good. I think we should go home."

As they head back down, Past-Me worries about his usually athletic dad who's sweating buckets. "Do you need some water?"

"I think I'll be fine. Been a long and tiring day. My mind's just a little all over the place with the project I'm working on."

"If you say so," Past-Me says, unconvinced. "Hey, if you're so tired maybe I can drive us home?"

I hadn't had my license very long and was looking for excuses to get behind the wheel.

"Sure," Dad answers.

And it's as if something in him changes.

Because, from out of nowhere, Dad brings up the most random thing, almost nonsensical at the moment. "I just want you to know that you are stronger than you think you are. I know you think that you are clueless about everything, but that's okay. Sometimes, it's fine to take advantage of that."

"Uh, where's this coming from?" Past-Me asks, almost laughing.

"Listen. It's okay to be a child."

"Dad, do you *not* want me to drive us home? Is that what this is about? Do you not feel safe with me at the wheel?"

"No." Dad laughs. "That's not it at all. I just wish you would understand that time can never be bought. Time can only be spent, and whatever precious time you've already used is gone, but you can still decide how best to spend your time in the future. You can choose to not go to college. I'm not going to stop you from making that choice. If you think you're going to have a better life doing something else, something artistic instead, we will support you as much as possible."

"Is this about me spending too much time on my games? Because I've put in a thousand hours on Skyrim and I still keep finding fun things about it. Also, did you clear the no college thing with Mom? Because I think she'd see things differently."

"Stop talking and pay attention! He's dying!" I scream at Past-Me. I can't believe I was being so dismissive, so clueless. It makes this even more unbearable, as if I'm slowly sticking a thousand pins into my body.

"Not about the gaming. And your mom still wants what's best for you. She still wants you to live up to your fullest potential, and not to compromise anything about yourself."

"Sounds all good and fine, but I don't want to be broke."

"It's not just about the money either, Hazeem."

They're back at the car, and that's when Dad clutches his chest. Makes a guttural sound Past-Me has never heard before.

"Oh God," I say, turning to Time, wondering if I should beg for this to stop. "I don't know if I can watch this again."

But Dad's collapsing onto the road.

And Past-Me can only stand there frozen.

Dad merely looks at him and says, "Come, Hazeem. Come closer."

Past-Me stoops down low, pulls out his cell phone. "What is it, Dad? I need to call 911."

"I just want you to remember one thing. This is the most important thing."

"Just let me dial—"

"Count not the years."

And then he's gone.

Time of death: 7:34 p.m.

CHAPTER FORTY-ONE

I exit the Chronosphere, ending up back at the house, in my dad's study.

Back in here again. Twice in one frozen day. More than in the past year.

"I wish I would have spent more time with him that day," I confess. "I wish I had done so many things differently. There was so much time wasted."

Time watches me as the Chronosphere floats next to them. "What would you change?"

"Everything. I'd do it all over again. Do everything with him. Even something as boring as reading the whole dictionary to him. Just to talk. And say the things I never got to say."

Time merely looks at me, with an expression that says *incomprehensible*. "We will never understand you."

A bitter laugh escapes me. "Of course you don't understand. You'll never get why it's so hard for me, yet I want it anyway. The pain I feel in my chest, at seeing his face again, as if he's alive, after having a lifetime of him suddenly ripped away from me. No, Time. You will never, ever, and I mean *never, ever*, know what it's like to be human."

Time's face changes then, but I can't quite read their expression. They whisper to the Chronosphere floating over their shoulder, before finally turning to me. "No one can change the past, so unfortunately that last day and your actions must remain as is for purposes of preserving the timeline. However, we can create a copy of the day, and insert you into it. So you can interact with it as your current self, in your former self." They pause, to let it sink in. "You can be with your dad again."

My heart nearly stops. "Wait—you can do that?"

"Of course. We're Time. We can do anything with time. Best not to think too hard about it. But bear in mind that this want of yours will render you experiencing his death once more. So it's not without its caveat. Do you really want it?"

I'm practically on my knees. "Yes. Yes, please. A thousand times over."

There's a glint in their eyes. "Be careful what you wish for."

With that warning, they simply snap their fingers, and I find myself back in the Chronosphere.

Facing a special black, edgeless gateway—seemingly made out of nothing but a hole with nothing visible beyond it—in the center of everything.

I stare at it, flabbergasted, because this is when things will change. But as I hold on to the precipice of the darkness, an uncertainty clamps my throat and silences me.

Yet, my feet continue to barrel through, into the black, taking me to the past that I need to confront.

To hopefully help me figure out how I can save everyone.

CHAPTER FORTY-TWO

The alarm goes off.

In the original day, I got up utterly bored, my mind already on my game.

But this time, the first thing I do is grab my phone and stare at the screen.

It's 6:45 a.m. on August 17.

A year ago.

I hop out of bed, leaving Mary to herself since she's fast asleep, and dash into the hallway.

Their bedroom door is open. I creep toward it.

And when I peek in, there he is . . .

My dad. Snoring away, with an arm over his forehead. His mustache bristling with every breath.

A quiet peace settles on me at seeing my old man. But I don't want to disturb his sleep, so I tiptoe away to the bathroom to take a speedy shower.

Then I fly down the stairs, to rummage through the pantry.

Pancakes. I'm going to make them.

The instructions are easy enough. I have all the ingredients, and the maple syrup is in the fridge.

Thirty minutes of wrangling with the art of cooking that would be lost on me if the box didn't have full instructions, and I'm done.

Plus, a quick brew of coffee in the pot on the stove.

When it's all ready, I take a glance at my handiwork on the dinner plate, grab the silverware, and set it all on a tray.

Something nags at me. Oh, that's right. The fact that my mom isn't around for any of this. But there's nothing I can do about it now.

Then I carry it all at a slow and steady clop, up the stairs, down the hallway, and into Dad's room, knocking on the door with my elbow. "Room service?"

His eyes flutter awake, desperately trying to focus at the strange intrusion, as he stares at the scene in front of him. "What . . . Huh . . ."

I make my way over and stare. The face I've missed for the past year looking right back at me. And something inside me melts. I can't believe I get to spend this day again, as I settle the tray on his nightstand. "I made you pancakes."

Dad rubs his crusty eyes, checks out the tray of food, then his son. "Are you okay? What's going on? Why aren't you downstairs, playing your games? It's the weekend, isn't it?"

I want to jump into his bed and give him the biggest hug, like

I used to do when I was four years old. "I just can't wait to hang out with you all day today. Think of it as a bribe."

"Why? What are we going to do?" Dad grabs the coffee and takes a sip from it. "Wow, nice."

"Ew. You didn't even brush your teeth."

"Coffee is a mouth cleanser. Don't tell your mom I said that. She has to kiss me."

"Ew again, Dad. I'll wait downstairs while you finish up and get ready," I say.

Dad stops sipping his coffee. "Wait. We're going this early?"

An ache tugs at my heart. I don't have a lot of time, so I want to make sure every second of this redo counts. "Can you just hurry up and eat and shower? Please?"

I still can't get over how healthy Dad looks. Even with that time bomb ticking away inside his chest.

There he is, with that grin, and those bright brown eyes. "You're being very weird today."

Now, when I look at his face, I see me in it. And when he smiles at me right then, my heart breaks entirely.

My dad is going to die today.

I hurry out the door and wait downstairs in the living room. Just staring at the wall. Because I don't know if I can do this.

But I must.

Thirty-seven minutes go by when his stomps on the stairs make his presence known.

"My son is so excited for today. I wonder why," Dad's booming voice says. "How about we just hang out together? Do some father-son activity, huh?"

"I have a better idea," I say, hopping off the couch. "How about if we pretend it's both our birthdays?"

Dad's forehead creases with worry. "Are you okay? You're not dying, are you?"

That question hits me square in the jaw, taking me more than a second to recover.

He looks even more confused as he scratches at the side of his mustache. "That's a joke, Hazeem. What is going on with you?"

"Nothing. I've decided to gift you the best gift ever."

Cut to . . .

"What're we doing at the hospital?" Dad asks, staring at the boring white building in front of us. "The last time we were here together was for your birth."

"This is my gift to you," I say, parking the car, then dragging a confused Dad all the way to the ER.

"Seriously, Hazeem. What are we doing here?" Dad asks again, more urgent this time.

"I just . . ." Honestly, I've no clue how to go about it. How will I even explain to a doctor—maybe the cardiologist?—that Dad needs surgery ASAP? "Just humor me, please."

I have to drag one extremely reluctant older man to the receptionist and try to explain the situation. But the girl behind the counter simply looks at me as if I've been muttering an ancient spell. She turns to my dad and asks, "Sir, do you share your son's concerns? Are you experiencing any symptoms of a heart attack? Feeling any discomfort or pain?"

"No, I'm not," Dad answers.

"But, Dad—"

"Hazeem, that's enough," he says firmly, before apologizing

to the receptionist for wasting her time. Then he makes me apologize, too.

She gives me a pitying smile. "It's okay. For what it's worth, I don't think you have anything to worry about. Your dad looks fine."

Dad doesn't look fine. He looks a little annoyed.

I feel the pointlessness of the situation creep into my soul. Finally, I march my way out of there, even though I wish I could tell everyone that Dad *is* an emergency.

When we step outside, Dad asks me, "What was that all about?"

I can only shake my head. "Nothing. Never mind. Let's just go to the beach." Seems as good of an idea as any.

"But you've always hated sand, calling it, and I quote, 'basically pointless powder.' Hazeem, what is going on? Seriously, did something change while I was asleep? Aliens came down or something?"

I rush us back to the parking structure. "Let's go to Malibu?"

"It's Saturday; it's going to be ridiculous there. And I have a deadline."

I want to ignore that word, especially at the knell that it sounds inside me. "That can wait. Please, Dad? Please?"

Dad stares long and hard at me, then finally gets into the driver's seat of his sedan. "Okay, I don't know where this is coming from. I thought teens hated hanging out with their parents."

"We're allowed to change our minds, y'know."

"Usually happens much later in life. Okay, Malibu it is, then. Even though I wish you'd clue me in a little on why you're being so weird today."

I smile at him, but it's forced, something to assure him that his son's still got it together. For now.

We spend the whole day at the beach, diving into the ocean water, afterward feasting on grilled fish.

I refuse to let Dad get anything fried, even as he smirks at me. "My own son. Forbidding me from getting fried calamari. What a travesty."

Then we head back to the beach and stare at the sparkling ocean. It's 7:29 p.m. Five minutes to go.

Dad starts experiencing the same chest pains.

I can only watch. "Dad, how do I get you to see a cardiologist?"

He doesn't know how to respond to the question. "I already have one. Your mom's friend. Best in the county. He gave me the green light two weeks ago. I'm beyond healthy. This is nothing."

Clearly, he's lying.

"Well, it's not nothing. You're in pain."

"It's probably just a little heartburn. It'll go away."

"No, it won't." I say, unable to look him in the eyes.

Even as he lays himself down onto the sand, shuffling around, trying to get comfortable. "Hazeem, listen to me."

"Dad, I can't." I still can't.

"No, please. Before it's too late . . . Remember, you're capable of anything. Anything you want to be. Today, I saw a glimpse of something new in you. Something that sparked you. I have no clue what it is, but all I have to say is . . ."

"Count not the years," I whisper to myself.

"Count not the years," Dad says out loud.

And just like that, my old man is gone.

Again. With me still feeling all sorts of cluelessness about what to do with my current situation.

Except . . .

CHAPTER FORTY-THREE

The alarm goes off.

I stare at my phone.

It's 6:45 a.m.

I'm back in my bed. Not back in the Chronosphere.

"Huh? Time? What is this?" I say.

Brown-furred Mary's in her plexiglass house on the desk like she's always been, as I stumble out of my room, only to stare at my parents' bedroom door, wide open.

A quiet shuffle with hesitant feet over to the gaping question.

Then my eyes settle on the sleeping figure, in that same position with the forearm over the forehead.

Dad. Same T-shirt. Same rumpled hair.

The date on my phone? August 17.

Whoa. What the . . .

Is this really happening—again? I tiptoe over to Dad, shaking him awake. "Are you alive?"

Dad shudders to life with a sputter. "Yes, oh my God, Hazeem. What is it?"

Is it actually possible? Am I reliving the day? Now what am I going to do? "I was thinking we could do something today. I could drive us. Maybe go to the museum?"

"That actually sounds kinda fun," Dad says. "I guess I can forget about the work I have lined up."

We both get showered.

Both head to the kitchen, where I make pancakes.

And both step into the same sedan in the garage.

"So, do you want to explain why you're derailing my plans for today, which I very gladly welcome anyway?" Dad asks.

"I just didn't feel like playing games all day, and I think it'll do you some good to not be in front of your workstation and tablet."

"When did you turn into Hazeem, The Wise One?"

I drive us to the Museum of Contemporary Art, and we explore the grounds for hours. Dad belittles some of the artists, talking big about his own graphic design skills. There are a lot of pompous exclamations of "I could've done that" and "That is literally a black circle with a blue line across it."

I listen to Dad without interrupting, letting all the sagaciousness sink in.

When we finally leave the museum, Dad says, "Okay, so we've played all day. I've got work to catch up on, Hazeem."

"That can wait. I just want to spend this wonderful Saturday with you. Is that wrong?"

Dad makes a pukey face, then takes a step back to avoid the

playful punch aimed for his gut. "No, I appreciate it. I truly do. Work can wait."

"I'm so glad you're artistic, Dad. What if I want to be like you?"

Dad makes another face, this time one that's unreadable. "Is that why we're here? Do you want to go to art school?"

"I have no clue about the future. I think I just want to have fun for a while. Not take life so seriously."

He swings an arm over my shoulders. "You know, as your dad, it's my duty to support you through everything. Even though your mom might say otherwise. But she's always been the most practical one in this relationship anyway."

"Okay, so I think we should go for an earlier dinner."

"Loving the random and fast-paced change of subjects, as if you're in a rush. Anyway, it's only five o'clock."

"Yeah, why not? Um, let's just go for a salad."

"Hazeem, you've never wanted—and I quote—'a cow's cud' ever, not a day in your life."

"I think it's okay to change my mind every now and then. Right?" Not if that means there's a chance a few leaves can save Dad's life.

"Let's go to Vegebites then. They've got some tasty seitan, in case you're feeling something a little meat-ish."

+ + +

After we've finished chomping down on our salads, I can't help feeling a little lost as we walk up Fairfax Ave, checking out the storefronts. "I don't know what to do."

"We can go watch a movie. Something we haven't done in a while," Dad suggests.

"No, not that." I don't want to sit in a dark room and not talk to him for two hours. "What if you knew there was going to be a disaster. Would you try to stop it?"

Dad takes a second to consider. "If I had the power to, sure. Why not? But it's impossible to predict the future."

"But what if you could?"

"Then do everything you can. Especially if the disaster may lead to the loss of lives."

I chew on the thought. I want to try and stop Dad's death, but there's no way to stop a heart attack.

We stop by a café to share a hot chocolate together, instead of getting one for each of us. Every single surprising thing I do brings sudden joy to Dad's face.

"I like this," Dad says. "I don't know what made you want to spend the day with me, but as your father, I'm feeling very grateful."

We are fifteen minutes away from 7:34 p.m. "Why do you think we're here?"

"I think we're planning to get your mom some pastries at that wonderful bakery on Third Street."

"No, I mean, do you think we can change our future?"

"Of course we can. Nothing is set in stone. Nothing is predetermined."

"But what if it already is?"

"I refuse to believe in that. I think Fate can't control anything and everything. I think Fate is fickle. And Fate always changes her mind."

I bump shoulders against him and he pulls me into his chest, and we fall into a natural rhythm we've not synced up to in years.

Yet Dad exhales the heaviest of sighs. "My son, why do I get this aura of heavy from you?"

"I just . . . I feel like I can't escape this . . . tragedy I'm in."

At 7:30 Dad lets out a major groan, then starts to sweat. And then he clutches his chest and lays himself on the ground. While bystanders start to gather around us, everyone concerned.

Even if I don't look surprised at all.

Once more, Dad whispers, "Hazeem, remember the most important words: Count not the years."

CHAPTER FORTY-FOUR

The alarm goes off: 6:45 a.m. on August 17.

Once again.

Pancakes. Again.

Then many visits to doctors.

Even calling 911 for the paramedics to get to wherever we are before his heart attack tramples its way through. Again and again and again.

Countless more to different holistic and spiritual therapists in LA. Very much to Dad's surprised face, his eyebrows hiked sky high.

I've tried an unfrozen, real-time, year's worth of different variations of this day.

One day, I convince Dad to let me take him on a cross-country flight on a whim. But only to places we can catch a flight to by 9 a.m. and land by 3 p.m. Pacific Time, so we can have a few hours together.

Just father and son.

We go to New York City. And get to eat tacos under the Jackson Heights subway station.

Then Cancun. To actually feel warm ocean waters, instead of the frigid dips at Santa Monica.

Then Puerto Rico, because why not? And also to have *arroz con pollo* and *maduros*.

Every single change I make to the day results in the same thing—Dad's expiration, the same best-by time of 7:34 p.m.

I cannot control destiny. But I keep trying.

After close to a thousand permutations of the same day, I've done everything I can think of, even after living through as many different days of Dad dying, again and again.

I realize I'm getting more and more numb to his death. And that's exactly what I'm trying to avoid.

Because I don't want to feel numb anymore.

I just want to feel.

Then one morning I try the unthinkable. I do nothing.

On that same August 17, after so many tries, even though my mind's still not tired of spending the day with my very-much-alive Dad . . .

I stumble past the sleeping Mary, then make my way to the same bedroom.

Dad's still in bed. The same position. Forearm over the forehead. And like always, the same Fahrenheit aftershave fills this space.

This is my dad, and there's nothing I can do to save him. So maybe we'll just do a whole lot of nothing together.

I creep on up, and shake the poor man awake.

"Oh my God, Hazeem. What is it?" Dad looks at me with bleary eyes and a huge question mark on his face.

"This is going to sound super weird, but remember when you used to let me sleep with you? Like a long time ago?" I ask.

Dad rubs the crack of sleep away from his eyes. "Yes, back when you were three. Until you told me you were too old to do that and wanted your own room and your own bed. Why?"

I don't quite know how to phrase the ask. "Can we go back to that? Just for today?"

Incredulous—that's the look Dad gives me when my words sink in. "Wait. Like, you want to crawl under the covers with me? Your dad?"

My nod is jittery and unsure, but I try to keep to a steady rhythm. "I just . . . I remember when I was little and Mom was working. And you would always cradle me and put me to sleep. I want to remember what that felt like, one more time."

"Hazeem, you're sixteen."

"I know. But can you please, just once, pretend I'm still three?"

Dad's silent for a good five seconds, seemingly unsure of the best response for what may be the new oddest moment in his life, paling those of the previous thousand mornings. "Well, then—says the old man, hoping for a proper explanation from his son—come on in."

Relief floods my body. "Okay, scooch on over, big guy."

Dad scoffs and shakes his head, but inches away, to his side of the bed.

For some reason, that acceptance and agreement by Dad means the world to me. And so, I dash over to my mom's side of the king-size bed.

And we just lie there next to each other, a gulf of two feet separating us.

"I'm sorry if I've been a bad son," I say.

Dad can't believe what he's hearing. "What? Hazeem, you've never been a bad son. Where is this coming from? And why the sudden urge to feel like you're three years old again?"

"Is it strange?"

Dad goes quiet for a moment. Somber. Another very long moment. "You know what. I think if more dads did this with their sons, the world wouldn't have the problems we're facing. Because toxic masculinity is vile, and starts at home. So—he says, as he tries to get over his bad dad morning breath—come over here and pretend you're a toddler again."

Dad pats himself on the chest.

At first, I'm clueless, because this is all so new. But then, I slowly inch my way over, then lay my head on his chest. And a pain instantly strikes me, as the only thing to fill my eardrums is the thunderous thumping of my dad's heart. The heart that will give way and fail mere hours from now.

Dad wraps an arm over my suddenly frail body. "So, you want to tell me what's going on?"

I raise my hand to my face, and for a moment, I'm filled with embarrassment at having to even talk about it. "It's just been kind of tough. I want to do nothing today. With you. The whole day. Is that okay?"

"Well, I do have to catch up with my sleep. And you know I'm a fan of sleeping in. You want to see how long we can just sleep here?"

"Yeah. Father-son bonding time of doing nothing. Plus, I know you can't leave me if I'm lying on your chest."

"I'll never leave you. You're the one who's planning to go to college and leave me in a couple years!"

Before I can stop them, the words escape my lips. "I don't want you to die."

Dad lets out a raucous laugh. "Where is this even coming from? I'm literally thirty-nine years old. Super fit. That's not going to happen anytime soon."

"We can all go anytime." I don't even know how to clue Dad in to the inevitable.

"Thank you, Mr. Morbid. Here, let me give you a superhug."

Dad squeezes me so hard I nearly lose my breath. Yet it feels good. Better than good.

And I let myself be enveloped by my dad's arms while imagining myself as a child once again.

I can't remember the last time I felt this safe. Just in Dad's embrace.

Mom rarely requested a hug from me, and definitely not since Dad died. But Dad is a totally different person.

I don't want to let go. Ever. "There would definitely be fewer wars if men got more hugs."

"You know what? I agree," Dad says, before kissing me on the forehead. "I'm going to be demanding hugs from you all the time now. Got it? And can I just say, I will love you regardless of anything. You're my son, and I will always be on your side. So if there's anything you are too afraid to tell me, just take a breath and let it out. I'm here to listen."

Oh God. Is Dad actually making me do it?

Well, guess it's time. Something I never got to do before. A deep breath in . . . and out come the words. "Dad, I'm gay."

Dad snickers, then kisses me on the forehead again. "Finally. I've been waiting for it."

"What do you mean? You've always known?"

He gives his most obvious "duh" face. "Oh my God. Hazeem, you talk about Jack so much, you don't even realize it. Then there are all the times you're busy texting him. Should see the look of utter contentment on your face. Sorry, Son, but I roll my eyes every time you're not looking. Glad you told me first, and not your mom."

Well, now I can't stop my cheeks from burning the way they do. "Why? Would she not accept me?"

"Of course she would! Your mom loves you as much as I do. I just like receiving preferential treatment from my only son. Call me selfish."

An ocean's worth of relief floods through me, drenching my insides, filling up my tear ducts, threatening to make each drop known outside of me. But I swallow it down. Because I'm about to ask the most important question of all. "Dad, what does 'Count not the years' mean?"

"Wow, where did you hear that one?" Dad's heart almost skips a beat but reverts to its natural rhythm.

"I think Nana might have said it one day."

Dad laughs. "It's my quiet, personal mantra. Something I came up with long ago, after my dad died. He wasn't the best person, and

I've always tried to break the hold he had on me, so I used it to remind myself that I shouldn't be chasing after regret. I shouldn't let myself stay stuck in the past. That time should not be our master. But that's not the entire phrase."

"What do you mean?"

Dad hugs me even tighter, and says, "Count not the years . . . but the tears."

CHAPTER FORTY-FIVE

What the— is the thought that flies through my mind, because all of a sudden, it makes so much more sense.

Dad's whole body starts quaking, but it's too soon for what I know is to come. When I prop myself up on an elbow, I see that Dad is crying, hard, eyes shimmering with tears.

"Dad? What's wrong?"

He wipes his face and takes a moment to collect himself. "I'm just so happy you feel safe enough to come to me, Hazeem. To have a moment like this together. I never told you the full story, but my father . . . it wasn't like this with him. He was abusive, in every way you can think of, to your nana and me, and I was determined to break that cycle with you. And I'm so damn proud of how you've turned out. I've spent so much time and energy fixing that broken part of me and rebuilding it, so you would never have to worry like I did. And now, your time is yours. We have a finite amount of it in this world. And we can either get stuck in the past, or we can do the things that mean the most to us. Just like this. This bonding time we're having has now become my most favorite thing ever. In the history of my life."

My insides are all raw at this admission. "I wish I had known. I wish you'd told me."

"That's my burden to bear. You're my clean slate. I get to shower on you all the positivity I've learned over the years. And be proud as I watch you grow up every single day. And I know life can be very difficult, especially for young people, where a whole year feels like a lifetime, but for me, I'm almost forty. A year is less than three percent of the life I've lived. In your case, don't rush. Have fun. And just like the saying goes, don't forget to cry. From happiness. Sadness. Excitement. Pain. Every tear is worth its weight, I promise you. It's a healthy thing."

I can't remember when I last did that, and I stare off at the white wall.

Dad looks at me—really looks at me—and continues. "I'm so grateful that you trusted me enough to come out. Is there anything else you want to tell me?"

After a year without him, I almost forgot how well he could read me—how well he knew me. Even in this fabricated reality, he knows. For once, I fear telling him the truth. I've lived this day so many times already, but I never thought to just tell him what exactly was happening. "Dad. I don't know how to tell you this. But . . . I'm going to lose you today."

He leans back slightly and gives me an odd look. "What do you mean?"

I pull away and lie next to him, shutting my eyes, wishing for the right words to say. "I'm going to try and explain it, and I know you won't believe me, but please, just trust me. See, I've been reliving this day again and again and again. Just like *Groundhog Day*, that movie you love so much. And every day you die of a heart attack. At exactly 7:34 p.m. We've done everything together, so many times. I feel like I'm getting to know you more and more every time I see you. And I love that I get to see you every single morning when I wake up on this August 17, but in the real world, you don't make it past this evening."

The silence that hangs between us is an impossibility to address.

"Wow, *Groundhog Day*, huh?" Dad's face takes on a gray shade. "But I believe you."

"You know I'm not a joker and—wait, you believe me?"

"Of course. I knew there was something off about today. You made that very clear."

I twist my body, so I can bury my face in his shoulder. "I've seen you die more times than I can count. Every single time there's been nothing I could do about it. We've seen cardiologists, given you herbal remedies. But nothing stops it."

Dad's strangely silent. He is handling all this so well.

"You're not . . . angry or anything? At your life being cut short?" I ask.

"Oh, my poor boy. Come here." Dad takes me in his arms again and holds me close. "The one thing I know is that I'm not afraid of dying. So even if it comes, I will be at peace with it. My only regret is not getting more time with you. Not getting to see all the amazing things you will do." Dad's voice breaks, and he collects himself before continuing. "But I know not to run away from death. We just cannot. It comes for us all eventually. And that's why it's so important for you to live your life to the fullest. As clichéd as that sounds. Don't go to medical school if you don't want to. Don't pick up art if you get bored watching me illustrate. Go travel, taste all the food, smell all the roses. And dance with Jack when you can, and if things with him don't work out, then with every other boy you meet. If there's a connection, ask if it's okay to kiss them. Let nothing hold you back. Especially not fear."

I bury my face again. Unsure what's going to come next.

"Now, I want you to take a deep breath," Dad says.

I do so.

"Let go," he says.

And the *whoosh* drags itself out through my tired lungs that have experienced a millennia of living. But it does. It comes out.

"Now keep breathing. Just in, out, in, out. Do you feel that?"

I can only nod.

"Let it out, my baby boy. Please know I'll never let you go."

And just like that, I shed my first tear since Dad's first and original death. Then it all comes out in an uncontrollable torrent of tears that my body has stored up since his death.

No clue how I had the strength to do that all along. But letting it all out helps my brain flush all the bad emotions with it, and my body is just racked with tremors as Dad tries to hold me close.

"It's okay. It's okay. I'm here for you. I'm always here for you.

Don't even think about what's going to happen. Just stay with me and let it out."

I mumble the words, "I'm scared. Scared of losing you again."

He lets out a slow breath of his own. "I'm scared of losing you, too. But I will always be with you. Through all of time."

CHAPTER FORTY-SIX

We finally fall into a long slumber together, father and son. Which now feels like the most natural thing we could ever do.

Serendipitously for us, I wake up just before sunset, as the sky outside turns to a beautiful creamsicle.

Only to find a drawing of me and him on my chest. Guess he must've gotten up for a few, and taken out his drawing pad and pencil from his nightstand, and sketched this out while I was asleep.

"Dad, it's almost time," I say, as I stare at his handiwork. The only new piece he's done since he died.

Dad wipes his eyes as he comes to. "Wow, did we sleep all damn day? We must've been tired. I guess I was, after that revelation," he says. The gravity about what's to happen hits us both. "You like it?"

I have no words. I can only nod.

"Want to hang out on the roof? Watch the rest of the sunset?"

"Yeah, let's do that."

Still holding on to the new image of me and him tightly, I make my way up the stairs and onto our roof deck, with him following along, silence hanging between us. And the view of the mountains ahead.

"I think I know my problem now," I say, still staring at the drawing.

"What is it?"

"I don't know how to ask for help."

"Yes, that is a problem, Hazeem."

I can only look at my feet. "I've been so busy trying to take care of people. After you died, Mom just drowned herself in work. I hardly see her, and she refuses to even talk to me. And Nana, I go to her place every day, just to make sure she's okay, since you're not around to do that anymore."

Dad's eyebrows knot together in deep concern. "That is a lot on your shoulders, Hazeem."

"You have no idea how much of a void you left in our lives. We love you, Dad."

"I love you all, too. But, Hazeem, you have got to figure out a way to ask for help. And to stop giving all of yourself to everyone, because eventually there won't be anything else left of you. Nothing left behind for you to live on. I don't think you understand when I say 'Count not the years, but the tears.' It doesn't mean just throwing away your entire life. You can cry for yourself, too. Not just everyone else."

Is that it? Sounds so simple when he says it. "I know that now."

"And you should do everything possible to make sure time is

not wasted. Not a second of it. Just know that you are deserving of a full life, that you are worthy of being loved by everyone, that you don't have to give away your time and your love to get nothing in return. Sometimes it's okay to be a little selfish. Love yourself, and you will learn how to love others."

Do I not love myself enough? "I don't know how to be selfish, Dad. You didn't teach me that."

"Maybe it's time to start thinking about yourself. Focus on you. And then you can help others. It's like that old saying about being on a plane, and they tell you to put on your emergency mask first before you put it on someone else. Because how can you take care of others if you can't even take care of yourself?"

"How are you able to make everything make sense?"

"Because I'm your dad and I'm twenty-three years older than you are?"

I muster a laugh. But my thoughts stay serious. "What if . . . what if I also die young? Like, at your age?"

Oh how Dad sighs. "Just because I die at thirty-nine doesn't mean you're going to die at thirty-nine, too. That's not how it works. There are a million different ways you can die before your time is up. You could get an aneurysm, you could get knocked down by a car, a toilet can fall out of a plane and squash you. But you can also live a full life as uneventful as drying paint. The point is, just keep living and don't be afraid of death. Because often if you live in fear of death, you're also afraid of living."

"What do you mean?"

"Well, take me, for example. I was always carefree. I was always living life. So wantonly that your mom would get annoyed at me. Back in the day, I even had a motorbike. And your mom wasn't very happy with it. In fact, she refused to ride it. Not even once. I loved it—that feeling of living on the edge. But the day you were born, I sold it off. I just could not bear risking my life and losing any time with you."

"But you die eventually. Or you will. Or you did." Why do I suddenly sound like Time?

"Yes, but I've lived a good life with you. Sixteen wonderful years. I wish we had more"—his voice cracks as he continues—"but if that's all I get, then I shall cherish them, even in the afterlife. I just hope you learn to live and to move on. Be with the ones you love, seek forgiveness, grant forgiveness, that sort of thing."

"I hope I'm strong enough," I say quietly.

"You know you are. I know you are." Dad sits there and stares at me, then grabs my hand. "I love you, Hazeem."

"I love you, too. Dad."

He shuts his eyes and lets the sun's rays continue to warm his face. "Remember, count not the years . . ."

"But the tears." The words escape my throat with a sob.

And with the stream trickling down my face that starts to fill my soul, taking away the emptiness, I finally say the one thing I never got to say to him.

"Goodbye, Dad."

CHAPTER FORTY-SEVEN

Once upon a today . . .

I find myself back in the house, with everything frozen, once again.

But something inside me is different. What used to be a gelatinous uncertainty has now firmed up, calcified into actual constitution, holding me up with its firm foundation. Spending all those looping days with my dad has changed me more than anything I've ever experienced before.

I guess it's because I finally have closure and, damn, that is a good feeling.

Time, always in their orange jumpsuit, is right next to me on the couch, petting the snow-white Mary Shelley in their hand. They're both staring at me. "How'd it go?" they ask.

Yeah, I'm curious myself, Mary Shelley says.

"I didn't think my dad could teach me anything else after he died, but he proved me wrong."

"What did you learn?" Time asks.

"That I won't be fine for a while. For quite a while, actually. But I have to learn to deal with it. Talk to people. Depend on people, that sort of thing. Eventually, I'll be okay. But I won't know when that will be."

"Quite the revelation from a single day's reliving. Well, if you think that for yourself, how about the timeline? How do we feel about that?"

"Well, I was thinking—"

"Always a dangerous proposition."

"—that maybe I can go back to a certain point in time and interact with people just like I did with my dad?"

"Yes . . ."

"Well, if I do that again, will it change today?"

"You mean manipulate the timeline?"

I nod.

Time shakes their head. "No. That can only happen in a different multiverse."

"Okay, but what if you unfreeze just three moments in our current timeline? This is the last thing I'll ever ask of you, and then it can all be over very quickly."

Time hops to their feet. "Too big of a risk. You could cause irreparable damage."

"What if you just unfroze people? Like you unfroze Mary Shelley."

Time thinks long and hard. "Does this mean . . ."

"I promise you, once I'm done, the timeline, you, this entire universe won't have a single anomaly ever again. Because I have my answer."

"Are you going to tell me?"

I shake my head.

The drilling stare from Time is the most unnerving, especially as the corners of their lips remain unmoving. "So, when shall we go?"

I think about everything that's happened.

About all the times I could have tried to change things.

I wish I could go back to when Jack was my best friend for life. And that we could figure out a way to say "I love you" to each other just like other friends do. To forge a new way through our friendship.

I wish I could go back to when Holly still remembered me.

I wish I could go back to Yamany and protect them forever.

But there's only one right time to go back to. The only thing that makes sense. "I want to go to their now. This very second."

Time thinks long and hard, then nods.

CHAPTER FORTY-EIGHT

Once upon a right this very frozen second . . .

Time raises a wagging finger at me. "Your actions on these three individuals will carry on. You will be stuck in your bubble of twoness with each one, but everything outside shall remain unmoving. It's up to you to deal with any adverse reactions they may have."

"Got it."

I exit the house I've always known and cross the street, calmly facing my challenge, seeing the shadow moving around upstairs.

I ring the bell, and it takes two whole minutes before the door swings open.

Holly sticks an eye in the two-inch crack. "Hazeem. What are you doing here?"

My heart jumps knowing that she fully recognizes me, name and all. But I try not to let it distract me. "I want to talk to you. And explain things."

"I can't. Something's wrong with my mom. She's not responding to me. She's just stuck with her phone to her ear, and I can't even make her move. I'm about to call 911." There's wild panic in her eyes, similar to how she looked the last time I saw her, after her accident.

"I know what's happening. Just . . . let me tell you everything that's going on."

The door clicks shut, then opens again, as Holly stares at me with that all-too-familiar face. She's propped up on crutches, but she is able to keep herself upright. "You know what's going on in this house?"

"It's actually the whole timeline. It's frozen. And it's my fault."

Holly's face goes slack. Then it crumples into one of utter disbelief. "Yeah, right. The timeline. Frozen. Because . . . what? *Star Trek*?"

I can't veer off course. "It doesn't matter right now. I wanted to apologize for everything."

Holly swings the door open, then gestures at me to come in. I scuff the soles of my shoes on the welcome mat and enter.

The house is exactly as I remember it.

We head on over to the dining room, and Holly takes a seat, settling her crutches against the wall.

"You look well," I say, to cut through the tension in the air.

"Thanks, yeah, my legs are getting stronger. My physical

therapist said a few more months and I should be able to walk without my crutches, at least for short distances."

"That's great," I say, meaning it. "On that subject I just wanted to say . . . I'm sorry. I should have tried harder to stop you, I should have just gone with you, I—"

Holly stops me by holding up a hand. She's silent for almost a minute before saying, "There's nothing for you to apologize for. It wasn't your fault. It was all me. If you had gotten in that car with me . . . I could've hurt you so badly."

"So, you remember?"

She nods. "It took a while, but eventually everything came back to me. For the most part, anyway."

We sit here for a moment in silence.

Then finally I say, "If you remembered, why didn't you ever . . . I mean, your mom told me you needed time to heal, so I didn't want to bother you. But I thought maybe once you were feeling better you would have texted or something. And when you never did, I figured you didn't want to speak to me again after I let you drive off like that."

"Hazeem, you didn't 'let' me do anything. I made a choice. You've always been so quick to place the blame on yourself—with what happened with Jack, and even your dad's death. And I knew you would do the same with me and I just . . . I was already dealing with so much guilt from my mom, I couldn't take yours, too. And it's no surprise that she took my phone away, hence, no more contact between us."

I hang my head. I'd been so wrapped up in my own shame, I never thought about how Holly was having to carry the weight of her own. "I'm sorry." It's the only thing I can think to say.

253

"I'm sorry, too. I should have just told you what was going on with me, but I guess I wanted to protect you, in a way. You were already going through so much." Holly takes my hands then, and I bring my eyes to meet hers. "You are kinder than anyone I've ever met, Hazeem. You're more worried about me than you are about yourself. I should have talked to you. I never wanted it to seem like I blamed you for what happened."

"I should have reached out, too. Seen how you were doing, seen if you remembered me. But your mom just seemed so adamant that I was hurting instead of helping, and I—"

"No need to explain yourself there. I know how scary my mom can be."

We both laugh at that, and it's like I can feel the weight lifting off of us both. I'd been blaming myself for her accident this whole time, when I really should have been blaming myself for not reaching out sooner. For letting my grief and guilt consume me. If only we could've gone through this whole ordeal together.

"I've missed you. I wish we could be friends again," I say.

She bites her lower lip, then shrugs. "I think it's time for us to be. Again."

I grab her hand and give her a big hug, which surprises her. "Wow, where's this coming from?"

"I've just missed you."

"I missed you, too," Holly says. "Now what was all this nonsense about the timeline?"

As I confide in her the silly truth about the sticky situation I'm in, it almost feels like a truckload of a burden has slid off my shoulders—now that I have patched things up with Holly. I know our path forward may be rocky for a while, but there's hope that it'll smooth out as we find our groove together. A new road toward re-friendship.

But I still have a lot of work to do.

Because next up is Yamany.

CHAPTER FORTY-NINE

I make my way to the library where they work. The same one I used to go to at least once a week before our whole world blew apart.

And there they are, at the counter. Staring at their colleague, who's frozen. Then at everyone around. Their face a mask of astonishment as they try to start a conversation, but failing miserably.

I make my way up to them, my heart pumping loudly.

Yamany looks at the only moving thing in their periphery and emits an audible gasp. "What are *you* doing here?"

"Well, you know, it's still my neighborhood library. And I've missed coming here."

Yamany nods. Then they look away, as if trying to escape this confrontation. "Something's wrong. I feel like I'm being pranked."

I don't bother looking over at anyone around, keeping my gaze fixed on them. "Can we talk? I can explain."

They hesitate for a moment before answering. "I don't know if we should."

"Please. I promise. It'll just be a few minutes."

They turn to a ponytailed woman next to them, wave their hand in front of her face, and signal at the computer as if to say they're going on break, then make their way around the counter.

"Let's just go to the park. I don't know who's eavesdropping around here. Even if no one can move an inch," they say, while side-eyeing all their colleagues.

I feel a tad guilty at that dig, which is also probably meant for me. "Best suggestion ever."

We exit the library and then follow the sidewalk that winds around the library, as cars are stuck on the streets and birds float overhead.

Yamany is filled with incredulity. "It's as if time has frozen."

"Yes, that's exactly it. And it's my fault."

"What?" Their eyeroll is the loudest thing out here. "You really think this is all because of you?"

I cringe at that one. "It's not that. I made some mistakes, and I need to fix them. Yamany, I don't know what to say to you other than I'm sorry. You were a really good friend to me, and I betrayed your trust."

Yamany sighs. "Thank you. I appreciate that. And as much as I don't want to admit it, I understand why you did what you did. You knew I was calling the Trevor Project, didn't you?"

I can only nod.

"What you did was . . . well, you were trying to be there for me,"

Yamany says, looking down at the ground as they walk, unable to meet me in the eyes. "I realize that now. But I didn't want you to think . . . ugh . . . I really don't know how to have this conversation with you."

I wait patiently for them to continue.

"I've been so conflicted about this," Yamany says. "See, I know you know what it's like to be gay. And I think you have an idea of what it's like for me to be nonbinary. And I know you also know that LA can be extremely cruel. Even though this is a super progressive town, it's not perfect. I was experiencing so much hate everywhere I went, it felt like. My mental health wasn't doing so good."

I want to interject, but figure it's best to stay silent.

"You being there in that moment stopped me from doing something really stupid. I realized after that I couldn't keep doing this alone. I wanted to be more open with you, but you were already going through your own trauma, I didn't want to pile more onto you."

"But that's what friends do," I say. "I'm not just going to give up on you because I'm going through my own stuff that I need to deal with."

"Yes, Hazeem, but you *weren't* dealing with your stuff. Moping around doesn't mean you were dealing with it."

"That's not fair."

Yamany shrugs. "It's true, though."

"You didn't have to stop talking to me completely, Yamany. Didn't have to recoil every time you saw me. I was so worried about you."

"I had to. I had to figure out my own things and give you space to figure out yours."

We let that percolate between us for a beat, to let it sink in.

Yamany continues. "I've actually been working up the nerve to text you, to be honest. I've been seeing a therapist, and lately she and I have been talking about how it would be good for me to have friends by my side through all of this. I'm so lucky to have my parents, but they can't replace someone like you. So, I guess what I'm trying to say is: I'm sorry for pushing you away."

I don't have words, so I just pull them in for a tight hug.

"So does this mean we can start again? Pick up where we left off?" they ask, voice muffled into my shoulder.

"Of course. I think we'll be even better than before," I say.

CHAPTER FIFTY

Two down. One more to go.

I stand a hundred feet from the flower stand at the grocery store, the same one from this unfrozen morning.

I have to do this. But my legs are like flan and my heart's drumming like an entire raucous marching band. Still, I make my way over.

Jack's still there, trying to spray down the overheating flowers. He hears the footsteps and does a quick head turn. And when he sees me, all he can do is sneer. Yet again.

My breath latches in my throat, the words dying on my lips, because I'm about to do it. I'm about to confront this boy. And finally, after much tugging, they stumble off my tongue. "Can I please just explain myself?"

Jack simply stands there, and even if he's bewildered by the frozen everything around him, he doesn't say anything about it.

"Look, I know things got really weird between us," I say.

Jack sneers again, refusing to say a word.

Seriously. What's up with him and the same damn sneer every single time?

But I don't care anymore. Because the whole universe is messed up and this is my last chance to change things. The script I had in my head disappears, and a new one flies from my lips. "You know what? That night on the roof, I wasn't just drunk. Ever since middle school, I had feelings for you that made me wish we could grow up to be more than just friends. And nothing's changed. In fact, it's gotten stronger, even though you want nothing to do with me. So what if you don't love me back and things will never work between us? So what if you're not my best friend anymore and I can't help feeling the way I do? Because the truth is you've always made me feel safe. Even now. I know that you don't have the same feelings for me. But I just want you to know that I have always been in love with you. That I am still in love with you. I wish we could talk, and you could tell me everything that's going on at home with your dad—"

At this, Jack really gets riled up, sneering even harder than before, before curling his lips down, about to launch into a tirade of a treasure trove of his unspoken words.

But I keep going. "I hope that things work out for you. I'm happy to respect your wish to never speak to me ever again. But I'm learning very quickly that we don't have a lot of time on this planet, and I want to make the most of it. Just know that I will

261

always love and respect you, and I will always want the best for you." I scratch at a sudden itch on the side of my neck. "I hope you'll give me a chance and you will want to become my friend again. Someday."

Jack stops sneering, and without saying another word, storms off into the grocery store.

I stand for a moment, alone in a frozen world once again.

Welp. I tried my best. Guess two out of three isn't bad?

I wait a little longer to see if Jack will return, but there's no sign of him.

And it becomes plainly obvious what my decision has to be.

CHAPTER FIFTY-ONE

We're back at the cemetery—me, Time, and Mary Shelley—with my nana thirty feet away.

Time rubs their hands. "So, this is it. We're going with Jack, aren't we?"

I look down at Mary Shelley in her backpack and stick my finger through a small gap in the zipper and stroke her fur one more time, feeling more at peace with my decision with each pet. Finally, I take the backpack off and lay it at Nana's feet.

I turn to Time. "Take me."

"Okay, that sniveling boy will be no—" Time screeches to a halt. "Excuse us?"

It's the only decision that makes sense. "I don't want anyone to lose their years. I want them all to live. None of them deserve it. So, it has to be me."

Time stumbles, almost falls to their knees. "What?"

I steal another look at Mary Shelley and Nana. I'm hoping they can take care of each other. Somehow. "Do it now, before I change my mind."

Time hops back up to their full height and paces the lawn. "Hazeem, at first we thought it'll be easy, but now, we realize it's not as simple as that."

"What do you mean? Just take me. And let everyone keep what they already have."

Time looks up and around them. "We will have to erase you entirely."

"Okay, I know that, and—"

"You don't get it. You see, every single thing in this universe, every single element, leaves a footprint. Which means I will have to take away *your* footprint, from the moment of your conception, so that we can salvage the timeline. It's the only way to get rid of your debt."

"So, you're saying no one will remember me?"

"Precisely. Every single trace of you, in every single timeline, will be erased. Every single instance of you, gone." Time gives me a peculiar look. "You're not willing to take back any of those years? Because you know, with our experience, having watched enough of your kind in this world, almost everyone would very easily and quickly take those years back. There's something about an unwillingness to die. Afraid to lose their life. They want to keep going for as long as possible."

"I know my dad told me to keep going, to always value every wonderful moment in my life. But he was happy with his short life— I can be, too. I think I've had a good run. I'm good to go. Literally."

"Is this what becoming an adult humanthing is like, because it's exhausting."

"My dad wasn't afraid. And I'm not afraid either. So, just do it."

"Are you one million percent sure?" Time asks. "Because this is irreversible. This will be your very last moment of being alive."

"Yyyyyyyyyyyyyyyeah." Ugh, that one word has to be dragged out of my lungs, my last shred of self-preservation making it quite the tug-of-war.

"Any last wishes?" Time asks, rubbing their hands together.

I think for a moment. "I wish I could have mended things properly with Jack. But I think I've left behind a good enough legacy with my friends. And my nana. I hope she forgives me for this."

"How about your mom?" Time asks.

"Uh," is all I can manage. It takes me a good moment to get to something proper and true. "I wish I could've had a relationship with her. Similar to what I had with my dad. But it's too late."

My gaze goes back out to Nana. I look out at her body, slumped over. She'll be so mad when she wakes up. But she won't even remember why she's angry.

"Goodbye, Hazeem," Time says.

My final, final, final words ever. The last thing I'll ever have to say. And then I'll be gone. My heart races, faster and faster, about to pop its way out of my rib cage.

I close my eyes.

Take a deep breath.

And slowly let it out.

"Goodbye, Time."

CHAPTER FIFTY-TWO

There's a moment when a flash envelops me, and then Time snaps their fingers. Not just once. But again, and again, and again.

I open my eyes and see Time standing there.

I'm right where I was before. "What's wrong?"

"Nope. You can't go yet. We just remembered . . . you owe us something," they say. "And we can't let you disappear before you give it to us."

"What now? I've promised to let you take me to fix the timeline. My life isn't enough?"

Time points to Nana. "Go take care of business with her first. We sense major hot flaming energy emanating from that woman. We think you call that 'furiosity.'"

Oh God. I don't know if I can actually face Nana. "Okay, just give me one minute with her, and then we're done. Got it?"

"We're done when we say so. Now, we shall unfreeze her so you can have the closure that you need. We shall stay in the periphery, so you won't be distracted."

I walk over to the last love of my life, getting to see her unfreeze in real time. "Nana? Are you okay?"

She blinks once. Twice. Then many times. "Hazeem. What are you doing?"

I launch myself at her, giving her the biggest hug. I've missed my nana, even though to her we were just together a few minutes ago.

"Why am I still here?" Nana asks, looking deeply confused.

"What do you mean? We came to visit Dad's grave. Remember? I think you fell asleep for a little bit. Are you okay? You're not feeling thirsty or hungry, are you?"

She shakes her head. "I thought I was done."

"Well, you were done with reading prayers for Dad."

She gets up to her feet and starts walking around. Staring at our surroundings. Then at me.

"Do you need my help?" I ask.

"I just want to see what's going on around here."

I trail behind her as she makes her way to the parking lot and then she goes up to everyone still frozen around us, and grabs their faces, one after another. "What is happening? Am I dreaming? Why does it feel like I'm dreaming? Something is wrong with the world. It seems like we're stuck. Stuck. I think that's the right word, isn't it?"

"I have to tell you something. We . . . we don't have much more time together. I'm going to miss you, Nana."

"I'm going to miss you, too," she says as she gives me a hug.

"I'm sorry that I won't get to see you anymore after this."

"Yes, me too," she whispers into my ear, and continues to hug me and hold me tight.

But something's odd. There's barely any resistance—and I haven't even told her what I'm talking about. "Nana, you do know what I'm trying to tell you, right?"

"I know. I hope you know that I know."

"Why are we speaking in riddles?"

"Hazeem. You know that it's my time, don't you? That is why it's confusing me right now. I shouldn't be here."

I take a step back. "Wait, what do you mean? It's *my* time."

Nana grabs me by the hand. "Let's just keep walking. There's some odd lady staring at us. Someone should tell her that color she's wearing clashes with every skin tone."

In the distance, Time watches in their neon-orange jumpsuit, suddenly concerned at Nana pointing their way.

I have to tell her the truth. No more confusing the sweet old lady. "I think I did something wrong, and I have to pay for my mistakes."

"You are going to have to do better than that, my grandson. You're going to have to explain to me everything."

"I don't know if you'll believe me."

"Try me. I'm not as old and dilapidated—no, decrepit is the right word—as you think I am."

And so I launch into a full explanation of exactly every single thing that's happened.

Me traveling back to the past. Me traveling the world. Me seeing Dad. Me living through the whole repeating day with Dad.

"Oh, it's like that movie *Groundhog Day,* huh? Or is it *Back to the Future*?" she says, as she tugs on the tail of her scarf.

"You don't seem fazed by any of this, Nana."

"I'm not," she says, before whacking me on the back of my head. "In fact, I'm furious."

CHAPTER FIFTY-THREE

Ouch, Nana! What's that pinch for?"

"For doing the stupidest thing I could ever think of." Nana leans against an SUV, fanning herself. "I'm not even hot, but you've got my blood pressure all the way up now. Why did you have to do a thing like that?"

"Like what?"

"Give me life. I was ready to go, Hazeem." Her face is filled with unimaginable rage. She's as red as a balloon about to pop.

In the distance, Time watches us with a meerkat-like curiosity, head bobbing around.

"But, Nana, I can't bear to lose you. I've already lost Dad. And I feel like Mom is long gone, too."

"It's not about you, Hazeem. It's about me. It's about what I want. I am ready to leave this Earth. Do you not hear me? I have lived on this planet for more than seventy years. And I can barely walk and all I want to do is to see my son. I want to see your dad. I have all the love for you and your mom in this world. But I am done. I'm tired. I'm exhausted. I've lived for far too long to have a seventeen-year-old boy decide that I should stay on this planet for twenty-two more years when I should not even be alive anymore."

I don't even know what to say.

"I was so ready to go," she continues. "And then your dad died. And I had to hold on, I had to stay on this planet for as long as I could to make sure that you were okay. It was the most I could do. And when I was done, you took that away from me. Do you not understand that?"

"I'm so sorry, Nana. I didn't know—"

"No, but do you not understand what you've done? To yourself? Hazeem, you've wasted everything you've been given by giving it to me. Me! An old woman who had already lived a full life. Why would you do something stupid like that? You chose to squander your life. I love you, but I do not want your years. Take them back."

"But, Nana, that means you'll be gone." And I'll still be here. Without her.

She spits on the ground, probably in disgust at the thought of having to still be here. "And I have every right to be. I do not deserve to live on this planet for two more decades. To be what? To live with other boring old people, and keep taking medications. Why keep me alive when I have accepted my fate? You are the one. *You.* A young man who needs to figure out how to keep living his life.

You need to figure out why you want to live a full life, a life bursting at its seams. Because I'm ready to die. Please understand that, my dear Hazeem. You were willing to give yourself up and I'm not willing to put up with that. And how did you do this? How did you make it happen? What kind of sorcery is this?"

"It's not magic. I told you, it's . . . Time."

"Hazeem, I've always been a modestly patient woman in my life. Trust me. Your dad had to bear the brunt of my anger because he refused to do what was best for his life and decided to become an artist. An artist! I didn't come all the way to America with twenty dollars in my pocket after my husband died, to teach your dad that he could just put coloring pencils on paper and hope to make his entire life worth living. But he proved me wrong. He ended up happy, and he had a wonderful family. So now you have to tell me how to take these years away, or I will try every damn day until I succeed."

The only thing I can do is to hold my nana, going in for a hug once more, but Nana's body is rigid. Steadfastly stubborn.

Finally, she gives in and limbers her spine, no longer erect. She whispers into my ear, "Hazeem, let me go. Please."

"I can't." I squeeze her tighter.

"You have to."

"I just don't know if I can, Nana."

"You have to live. Let go of the dead and *live*, my poor boy. You have suffered enough. You should no longer put yourself through this. You are deserving of so much love—and life—for yourself. I wish I had the desire and the will to want to keep living. So, find it for me. Find it for yourself."

And just like that, my resolve wavers. I was so sure I was

fine with being erased. And now, listening to her, I'm torn all over again. "Are you sure, Nana? Are you sure it's going to be okay?"

"I have never been more certain in my life. I love you, Hazeem. Now, it's time for that weird woman staring at us to fix this."

CHAPTER FIFTY-FOUR

Come over here, you!" Nana yells over at Time.

Time looks at us, then all around, and screams, "You can see us?"

Nana rolls her eyes. "Of course I can. I said, come here."

Time sprints over with the Chronosphere in hand, then tucks it away.

"What's that metal ball you just had?" Nana asks.

"Just a record-keeping device that, you know, keeps a documentation of everything that's happening all the time."

Nana looks unimpressed. "My grandson says you're responsible for everything that's happened."

Time gives a flourish of a bow. "Not quite responsible for it, but we are its caretaker. And your grandson here has quite a bit of a mess that we've been helping him figure out."

"I hear you are in need of some reparations? Whatever it is that my grandson has given me, I need you to take it back and give it to him. I don't want it."

Time looks somewhat relieved. "Ah, well, that's a strange twist to this problem. Hazeem, did you ever think to ask those people you've given those years to if they wanted them?"

"I thought they were a given . . ."

"Yes, but were they a-wanted? Because now your grand-nana is saying that she does not care about receiving any."

"Next time, I'll check first," I say, with a very intense heating up of my cheeks.

"There won't be a next time, oh young one. Remember?" Time says with a violent shake of their head. "Okay, does this mean we can get things moving?"

"Just . . . one more second, please," I say, turning to Nana. "I love you so, so, so much. You were the best grandma a boy could have ever asked for. And I'm so glad you gave me my dad. Because the two of you were the most important people in my life."

Nana sighs. "Hazeem, do not forget about your mother."

"She's the one who has forgotten about me."

"You have to make her remember. You have to explain to her that you need her right now. And you cannot just let her overlook you."

"How?" It's the only word I can muster.

"You will find a way. You are the strongest boy I've ever met. Stronger than your dad ever was. Your dad thought with his heart and you think with your heart, your brains, and your gut. You have good instincts—listen to them. But one thing you both will have in common is a full life, regardless of how many years you live. And

275

I remember your dad; he was not afraid of dying. I know even on the day of his death there was no fear in him. He was ready for anything that happened. And you should be ready for that, too."

I can't seem to let go of her, my hug threatening to choke the life out of her body before Time can take it.

"Just in case Time here decides to play you dirty, I'll come back and haunt them for eternity," Nana says.

Time takes a step back, both hands on their chest. "Oh no, no, no. We follow the rules. We live by the metal ball. We know to do everyone right."

"I don't understand the concept of time. But I do understand what I'm looking at right now. And it looks like you're a fan of all sorts of games, and I certainly don't want to hunt you through time," Nana says.

"There will be no need!" Time assures her. "Now, if you're ready . . ."

I release my nana but hold on to her wrinkly hands. My heart is torn to fifty pieces, but I'm slowly learning to stitch them all back up. One by one. "Goodbye, Nana." Then I give her a kiss on the cheek.

"Now. Where's that chair?" she asks, as we make our way back to Dad's grave. She grabs the same seat and plants herself on it.

Then she takes a slow breath, lets it out, and says, "I'm ready."

Time simply snaps their fingers . . .

And her wish is granted.

CHAPTER FIFTY-FIVE

I sit there next to my nana.

The first thing that hits me is how loud the world is. Even the breeze rushing against blades of grass sounds like a jackhammer to my ears. Ears that've been accustomed to eerie quiet for several lifetimes.

Nana's eyes are closed, and she's leaning against me on the chair. And even though she's the smallest woman ever in my eyes, her body weighs me down, draining all my strength away with every passing second.

She's gone.

And I have not stopped crying since the moment she let out her last breath.

What do I do now? "Does this ever get easier?"

Time merely shrugs. "We can't predict your future. Sometimes you humanpeoples are capable of surprising us still."

I can't get over that it's just me now. Even though I've traveled to the ends of the earth with only Mary Shelley as a companion, I've never felt more alone.

"Shall we play a little game?" Time asks.

"I'm not really in the mood."

"So what do you want to do? Just sit there?"

"My grandma's just died, so yes. I'll do just that."

"But it seems like everything's back to normal. Isn't it?"

Trees sway in the breeze. Birds chirp around me. Cars fight against traffic on the street out there. The silence is definitely gone.

Everything's back to normal. Except for one thing.

Me. I'm no longer who I used to be.

But before I can delve any deeper into my feelings, I hear my name being called.

It's my mom, rushing over to me, looking exactly the same as she did this morning.

My throat tightens. She actually made it. But seeing her does not put me at ease at all, even though I know she's the only adult who knows how to handle what's happened to Nana.

She's twenty feet away, closing in. "Hazeem? What is going on? Why is Nana sleeping—"

When she gets close enough to see my face, tear-streaked and swollen, the realization hits her hard. She dashes over to Nana and drops to her knees, grabbing a wrinkled hand and checking for a pulse.

"She's gone," I say.

Silence. Mom's brows furrow more intensely.

The quiet between us is killing me. "She's passed away. I was right here when it happened."

My mom looked this harried only once before.

I still remember her on the day my dad died. She made it all the way to the park, just seconds before the coroner's van took him away. She was holding it in, trying so hard not to break.

She's doing it again now. "Are the paramedics on their way? Why didn't you call me?"

I shake my head. "I don't know what to say to you, Mom."

"You'd tell me Nana's in trouble, and—"

"No, I don't know how to say anything to you! We don't talk. We haven't since dad died."

She purses her lips, then hangs her head.

That's when her body quakes. And a tear rolls down one cheek.

But before she can even sit in those emotions, she's back on her feet. "I've got to make the funeral arrangements. She has to get an autopsy, and all that legal stuff. Everything will be taken care of."

Of course. Because she's going to make sure of it. She's already on the phone. An intense hive of activity all abuzz in one person.

And before I know it, the paramedics are here. What an odd place for them to be, seeing how a cemetery already holds the dead.

But it's causing a commotion as a group of curious onlookers start to hover around us, trying to catch a glimpse of this old woman who has just left our world.

My mom returns, casting a strange look at the crowd. "Okay, so the funeral will be held tomorrow."

All I want is a cup of water. I feel like I've been crying for so long, there is no moisture left in my entire body. And my skin is flaking away into dust, leaving behind a desert of bones.

"Hazeem, are you okay?" my mom asks.

"No, I'm not. I feel like we're running out of time."

She looks like she's about to give up on everything, her eyes drilling hard at nothing in her direct vision. "Can you be more precise with your choice of words? I don't understand what you mean."

"I don't really know how to explain it to you. I don't think you'll believe me."

"Try me," she says, taking the seat that Nana had occupied just minutes ago.

I look in the distance, at the body bag on the gurney being wheeled by two female paramedics. "When Dad died, you withdrew from me. Why'd you do that? Why'd you abandon me?"

She looks up at the sky as if the answer may be written up there, but there are no clouds to clue her in to the right answer. Finally, when her eyes stop roving the heavens, she turns to me and says the most unexpected thing.

"Because when he died, I died, too."

CHAPTER FIFTY-SIX

Mom lays her hand on mine. "It's just been so hard. I was so in love with your dad and I just . . . I'm still trying to pick up the pieces, to live with the fact that he's gone. Every single day."

It's hard to stay angry with her when she said so clearly what I've also been feeling. "I've never felt so alone in my life," I say quietly.

"I'm so sorry, Hazeem. I just . . . didn't know how to take care of myself, so I had no idea how to take care of you. The only thing that seemed to stay the same was work, so I poured all of myself into that."

I don't know if my eyes are capable of pleading, but it seems like they are doing just that. "But you can barely look at me, even now."

Her eyes dart up to mine for a moment before she looks away again. "You just look so much like him. But without that annoying mustache he loved so damn much," she says. We almost laugh at that. "Sometimes it's easier for me to turn away than face things head on. Why do you think I've been leaving you to your grandma this whole time? Because I don't have the strength that your father had."

"I don't know if I do either. But I need your help. And I know you need mine. Now that Nana's gone, we only have each other."

Mom's face turns ashen. As if everything she's hearing is sinking in. "Have I been that bad of a mother?"

"No. But you can't just leave me alone, to fend for myself."

My mom grabs my hand and stares deep into my eyes. "Hazeem, I was filled with so many bad thoughts that I had to keep them to myself, so I didn't poison you with any of it. Now, I don't know if we'll ever get over this, but we're going to get through it, together."

"I . . . I . . ." Is this possible? Are we not too broken?

Her gaze has not left my face. "Just . . . just give me time. I need to relearn some things. But I promise you I will not let you go."

The very same words my dad had said.

She wraps her arms around me—it's awkward at first, but we settle into it—and cries into my shoulder. "How are you such a good son?"

A part of me is reluctant, but this feels safe. And I think I'm finally in good hands. I coax the words, and they come out naturally. "I love you."

She's silent for a second, as she kisses my forehead. "I love you, too, Hazeem." Then in the next heartbeat, she says, "You know how we can start? By me coming home for lunch every day. And when you're back in school, then we'll spend either all of Saturday or Sunday together. How does that sound?"

A warmth spreads itself throughout my body. "Perfect."

CHAPTER FIFTY-SEVEN

The house is quiet as my mom and I make our way in. It's just the two of us. Which is weird, because I'm so used to having been with Time, too, now. God, I was with them for barely a second, but it was an eternity of a second.

Suddenly, I miss their presence.

But I have to focus on my mom. Because we have to work together now.

And so we do. We're going to have people in here tomorrow to celebrate Nana's life. We divide up the chores and start cleaning up, trying to set things right. Not just for the house but between the two of us.

We move through the whole gigantic space. The living room. Kitchen. Garage. In no time flat, we're pretty much done.

But there's just one more thing I need to do.

I make my way into the garage, climb up to the rafters, and lift out all of Dad's boxes that contain his paintings. Then to his study, to grab the remainder that are stored in there.

I quietly bring them into the living room. Mom looks at me, at them, then sighs. "Let's do this."

Together, we return every one of his paintings back to its original location.

When we're done, the house finally feels like a home again, especially with its explosion of colors, oh-so-warming and truly inviting.

We reach a point when there's nothing left, when everything that needed to be done has been done, and Mom makes her way to the kitchen.

She calls out, "Hazeem, would you like some lemonade?"

I join her, and sit at the island. "That sounds good."

After pouring us a glass each, she grabs the stool on the opposite end. And we're just staring at each other as we sip our tart drinks.

Then she reaches out and grabs my hand. "How did you get so big? What did I miss this past year?"

"I've been the same. Don't think anything's changed."

"No, something in you is different. My boy used to be so carefree. You used to laugh at everything. I don't remember the last time I heard you do that," she says, looking genuinely concerned. "Is there anything you want to talk about?"

It'd be easier to just tell her everything is fine, to keep everything deep inside like I've been doing. But she's asking. And she's looking at me like she's trying to see me. So, I try.

I spend some time explaining to her all that happened with Holly and Yamany . . . and Jack.

"I didn't know you felt that way for Jack," she says plainly.

"Is it . . . okay?"

"What? Of course! Your dad and I, we always had a feeling. Even back then, I noticed you act differently with all the kids around. It was as if you were jealous. Because boys and girls are always allowed to like each other. And it was kind of obvious that you felt differently than them."

"Oh, was it that obvious?"

"A mother's intuition is always right," she says, a newfound lightness in her voice.

"It doesn't matter anyway," I say with a small shake of my head. "Jack doesn't even want to be my friend, let alone anything else."

"Give him some time. Like you said, maybe there's something going on with his dad. Things may be difficult for him."

I nod but keep my eyes trained on my glass of lemonade as it sweats onto the granite countertop.

"Hey." Mom reaches out to grab my other hand. "You are loved, Hazeem. You do know that, right?"

I squeeze hers right back. I'm starting to realize it with every passing second.

CHAPTER FIFTY-EIGHT

I must have slept in late because by the time I open my eyes, the clock says ten o'clock. Wow, I must have been exhausted.

But it is a new day.

It's quiet all around. Almost as if I'm the only one in here.

Even Mary Shelley's asleep, as she always is.

So I comb through the house, searching for my mom, but she is nowhere to be found. Her door is open, but the room is empty.

Would she really have left me on the day of Nana's funeral? After everything we said yesterday?

But then the door to the garage creaks open.

And there she is, looking more tired than ever. "Sorry, just had to stop by the mosque to take care of your nana's body. We'll head over there for the funeral once you're ready. And then if anyone wants to come over afterward, they can—oh, hello."

Mom is surprised when I wrap my arms around her in a hug. She's still here.

She kisses the side of my head. "How about I go make us a quick breakfast?"

"Sounds good," I say, letting her go.

I'm about to run upstairs to shower when the doorbell rings.

What welcomes me as I swing the door open is the most surprising sight: Holly and Yamany.

They launch themselves at me and silently whisper how sorry they are about my grandma.

"How'd you find out?" I ask.

"Your mom stopped by the library to tell me. So, I decided to come by, see how you're doing," Yamany says. "Then I bumped into Holly here, hovering outside."

"Yeah, I wanted to say hi. But I found out what happened from Yamany here. So glad we finally got to meet," Holly says. "And also, I really wanted to talk about yesterday. You know, the weird event."

"What? Like, time being frozen?" Yamany laughs, but stops. Because Holly's face is just . . . "It happened to you, too? So, it *was* real."

Mom's in the background. She watches the three of us with a smile on her face.

"Come in," I tell them. "I've got to finish getting ready to go to the mosque. We can talk all about the . . . frozenness . . . later."

"We can come with you? Is that allowed?" Holly asks.

I grab both their hands. "Of course. That'd be nice."

Mom leads them both to the kitchen while I head upstairs. In the bathroom, I take a moment to stare at myself in the mirror. All I can think of is how thankful I am. That I don't have to be alone today. And that I have the people I love, people who love me, by my side.

After I quickly shower and get dressed, I make sure to feed Mary Shelley some baby carrots, then head back downstairs, where my mom has already served some wonderful chai. She's draping the most floral of headscarves over Yamany's and Holly's heads, to show respect at the mosque. Even though my two friends have never really spoken to each other before today, they've clearly hit it off, as they compliment each other on how good they look in their new headwear.

Mom spots me and asks, "Ready to head over?"

"Ready," I say. And I mean it.

✦ ✦ ✦

At the mosque there's already a procession of a few dozen congregants. See, when we die, everyone familiar to our family stops by to offer their prayers and farewell.

It's the last time I get to see my nana. As I kneel next to her body, I whisper a quiet prayer for her.

And then that's it.

The procession carries her body onto the hearse. And together, we make our way to the cemetery, the same place I was at yesterday. Where my life changed in unexpected ways.

Yamany, Holly, and I ride with my mom, while a few dozen other people follow along. They join our side and mouth words of condolences at the cemetery. My nana is laid to rest next to my dad, so that mother and son can finally be together again.

Her wish granted.

My mom hugs me and plants a kiss on my forehead.

I can't help but look up at the sky, wondering if I could be as happy and at peace as Nana is today.

But I'm hopeful, as I look at everyone around me. My mom, Yamany, Holly . . . all three of them forming not just a rock but a mountain for me to lean on.

And so as we make our way back to the car, I hold hands with Holly and Yamany, and together, we fall into a steady rhythm. One that will hopefully never get out of sync.

"Do the three of you want to grab some pizza and bring it back to the house for whoever wants to stop by?" Mom asks.

"Yes, I like that plan," I say.

Maybe things are headed toward normal for the first time in a year.

Although, there's still that one nagging thing about me owing Time something else, according to them. But they're nowhere to be found, so maybe that's a good thing?

CHAPTER FIFTY-NINE

It's weird having people from the mosque here at the house—
some of them Nana's friends, some Dad's, and some Mom's.

The mood is kind of somber, but I guess everyone is trying to
make do with the fact that our tiny family has had two deaths in
just a year's time.

No surprise that everyone's giving me a wide berth. The boy
who has lost his dad and his grandma in such a short amount of
time.

But Yamany and Holly are by my side, trying to talk to me and
distract me from things. I have to constantly assure them I'm going
to be fine, but it's not annoying at all. I'm happy they're here.

Holly says, "I would love for the three of us to get to hang out
again soon."

"Seeing how you've never even bothered to introduce us in the past, Hazeem," Yamany says, teasing but with a sharp truth in their words.

Oops. I knew my separate worlds would have to come crashing together someday. I didn't imagine it being the day of my nana's funeral, but perhaps this was how it was always meant to be. Both of them here for me on the day I most needed it.

There's a flicker of movement in the corner of my eye. And as I turn my head, my throat seizes at seeing a flash of orange.

Uh-oh.

"What is it?" Holly asks.

"Hmm . . . Can you give me a minute? I just have to go talk to someone," I say.

I make my way to the living room. And there they are.

Time's back in their neon-orange jumpsuit, hovering by my mom, who's busy talking to the imam.

Not at all concerning.

But then Time quirks an eyebrow at me and wanders through the house, then shoots a glance over their shoulder.

As if they want me to follow.

And so I do.

I wander through the hallway and into the kitchen, and Time is right there. At the back door.

"Why are you here? I thought we were done," I say, pretending like I don't remember the mysterious thing I apparently still owe them.

"Not yet. I'm here to collect." Time doesn't say anything more. Simply disappears through the door, appearing on the other side.

"Okay, you're acting really weird," I say. "Do I keep following you?"

Time nods and juggles their Chronosphere.

"I don't know what's going on. Are you playing a game with me?"

As I make my way through the back door, it's obvious something's not quite right. I fear the floor may open up beneath my feet any second now.

They lead me to the backyard where I notice a presence. There's a shadow there, just outside the guest house. But why would someone be out here?

As I make my way over, I see a figure, with their back to me. Dressed in a crisp shirt and pants.

Oh. I never thought I would see this, ever.

Time simply looks annoyed, before winking out of existence.

Because the person turning around to face me is the last person I would expect to see.

Jack.

CHAPTER SIXTY

Jack's beautiful face freezes me up all over again. I just can't help staring at those gorgeous brown eyes and those sharp cheekbones that demand actual blood from my fingers.

As he drills a stare at me, I'm suddenly all wobbly.

But it's almost as if I'm looking at him from a different perspective. I've lived lifetimes with only Mary Shelley by my side. And if there's one thing I've learned from all of this, it's that the people you care about is what makes life worth living. I will always care for Jack, but if he doesn't feel the same for me, I'm ready to accept that.

I brace myself for whatever he came here to say.

"Hazeem, I'm sorry," Jack says in a rush.

Uh. I wasn't expecting that. "What?"

"I'm sorry for ignoring you this whole time. Especially after your dad died. And I'm sorry about your nana."

"Oh. Well. Thank you."

We're silent for what feels like forever.

"Um, I have people waiting for me inside so . . ." I turn to go, not expecting more from this conversation.

"Wait!" Jack takes a deep breath, then launches away. "Do you remember what you told me when you were drunk? Then again yesterday, when time seemed to have frozen itself, which I thought was super weird, but that's not the point."

Oh my God. How the hell can I forget? "Umm . . ."

"The point is . . ." He's not sneering this time, but actually blushing. "I can't stop thinking about it."

I wince. "I'm so sorry for putting that on you. I totally understand it wasn't cool and—"

"Oh my God, will you just shut up?"

Yikes. Shut up, I shall.

He scratches his shaven head, cracks his knuckles, tugs at his collar, makes a face as if all his flesh and bones are too tight for the skin he's grown up in. "I can't stop thinking about that night because I can't stop thinking about you."

It's like time has stopped all over again.

"Our friendship was so special. It was different from the others I've had. And to suddenly realize why it felt different, it was unnerving. And I don't know if my dad would be very welcoming of you—of us. He's so obsessed with me carrying on the family name and marrying a nice girl from Yemen. But I should be following my heart."

He makes his way over, narrowing the distance between us and grabbing my hands.

The warmth of his touch, suddenly giving me life.

"So, what are you trying to say?" I ask, my throat dry.

"I had to protect myself from you. From my . . . feelings for you. And that's why I've been staying away, because I was so scared. I was so scared of giving in to you. I have been so miserable this past year and falling off the roof that night and looking up at you from the ground, I think something changed in me."

I want to interrupt him so badly, but I'm so afraid of spooking him, I keep my lips firmly sealed.

"Remember how you came to the store yesterday to talk to me? Well, last night, I had the worst fight of my life with my dad. He was ready to send me back to Yemen today, so I can meet a nice girl, and get married, and bear him a boy. But I don't want that. Not while I'm still trying to figure things out. Not after you . . . said those things to me."

I'm clueless about what to do or say next. So I simply blurt out, "You can come stay with me. We have this guest house. It's empty."

"No, no, that's not why I'm here. I'm moving in with my coworker. I just . . . I want us to hang out again. No, actually, I want to do more than just hang out with you. I want to be more than just your best friend. I want to go back to that, *plus* some more. See, when my dad first told me that he wanted to send me back to Yemen, I was about to text you that I didn't want to leave."

Yeah, how do I tell him that I saw the text?

"I was too scared to finish that sentence. I didn't want to leave this country, but more importantly . . . I didn't want to leave *you*. You are my family. And I want you to know, I love you right back, Hazeem."

Okay, I just died.

Because that's the biggest twist ever in my whole entire life. I'd been pining after Jack for so long, I never even considered he might feel the same way. "WHAT?"

"Why are you shouting at me?" he says. "Anyway, now that you know that, I want to finish what you started on that roof."

He leans in with his eyes closed and taps his lips onto mine.

Just a tap, as I stare at his face. His nose touching mine.

Is this real?

And for a moment I'm lost. Lost to everything in the world. Lost in time because this boy is making me feel things I've never felt before.

I have so many reasons to want to live now. And this is just one more. Yet, I pull away because something bothers me. "But I thought you hated me. You were always making this sneering face—"

"Wasn't it obvious? It was so painful to look at you because all I wanted to do was hold you or kiss you. I'm sorry it took me this long to figure things out. So, are we going to be okay?"

The smile that creeps onto my face is a welcomed stranger, and one I have to get to know more. "I think we can give this a try."

He reaches out to stroke my face, and that's when I notice it.

The scar on his palm. Which looks like a 7.

Why's it so familiar? Almost as if I've seen it before. "How'd you get that?"

He glances at it. "When I landed on the ground after I fell from

297

the roof, there were broken bits of the Bud Light bottle everywhere, and I accidentally cut my palm. I needed five stitches, but, yeah, it wasn't your fault."

"Huh." That's all I can say, as I vaguely remember a sailboat and—

But it's too late, as he swoops in for a kiss.

And I die all over again.

CHAPTER SIXTY-ONE

We start heading toward the house (after a sufficient number of kisses) when I see Time again, on the sidewalk across the street. "Give me one second. I've got to go talk to someone. I'll see you inside? Make sure you ask for Holly and Yamany. They'll be super excited to meet you."

I leave the comfort of Jack's warm hug and watch him disappear through the back door. Then I march over to Time, to give them a stern talking to. "You could have just told me he was here."

"And spoil the fun," Time says, with brows furrowed. "What would be the point of that? So, are you going to be okay?"

"I think I will be." I do have to ask the question that's been bothering me. "Are we squared away?"

Time looks hesitant. Something's still wrong. Yet they remain silent, just staring.

"Tell me what's wrong. Please. I think I've done everything right, like you wanted me to."

"You still owe us one thing," they say. They open their arms wide, and I wonder if we're about to take off somewhere.

But then I realize. It's so obvious. So simple.

I pull them toward me and wrap my arms around them. "You are Time. A being who doesn't know how to be human. But this should hopefully give you a good idea."

Time is quiet as they pull away. Ruminating. "Too troublesome. We would never want to be human."

"That's okay. I'm still glad I met you."

"We are, too," Time says, "and the Chronosphere says they are happy as well. We are happy."

"Happy? So you're saying I did that. Made you feel an emotion?"

"Don't get your head all in a bundle."

A sorrow carves its way through my chest. "Will I see you again?"

Time's still for a moment, as if thinking, then takes a step back before blinking out of existence.

Wow. That's a little sudden, even for a departure.

Until I feel a presence behind me. I spin on my heels and—

There's a strange man, with skin as brown as mine, but hair nearly gone gray—definitely older than my dad—standing there. Just ten feet away. But he looks kind. Full of understanding. And familiar.

The familiarity is what's killing me. "Are you one of my nana's friends? The remembrance is right through that door over there." I point to the back door that Jack's just gone through.

He shakes his head, before smiling the warmest smile. "Wow, I can't believe I get to see you again. Meet you again."

"What do you . . . I don't remember ever . . ."

Why does he look so damn familiar? And why does he have that nose, those eyes . . .

Those eyes. The same eyes—

"Who are you?" I ask. "Tell me right now, or I'll—"

"You know who I am, Hazeem."

One more glance. I can't deny he is who he is.

Because suddenly, the image of him on a sailboat, with the dashing man who has the scar on his palm that looks like a 7, pops into my mind. "You . . ."

He nods. "Yes. Me."

I can't help the dryness in my throat. "Are you . . . me?"

He nods again. "You asked Time if you will meet them again. We do. Just once more, though. And it's for this moment."

I'm confused. "They brought you from the future? Brought you here to the past? To see me? Why?"

He takes several strides toward me, until he's a mere arm's length away. "Because they wanted me to give you the biggest gift anyone could."

"What is it? Don't tell me it's a billion dollars."

Future-Me laughs. "Not quite. Just . . . this." He leans forward and wraps his arms around me. Pulling me in, letting my head rest on his shoulder.

And I respond the only natural way I can, by wrapping my arms around him. I can't even stop the release from my throat, a gentle exhale, followed by a strangled sob.

"This," he says, "is what it feels like to love yourself."

And the tears are freely running down my face again. Words are lost to me.

He continues. "Dad dying really screwed us over, didn't it? And emptying out our heart, carving all that space, so we wouldn't ever get hurt again, didn't help us either. It'll take us a while to trust that we're capable, and for us to get to a happy place. But just know that I love you. Everything we went through took a lot of that self-love and feeling of worthiness away, but eventually we will fill it up with all the joy we find from friends, and family, and the stories that we will tell everyone who's willing to hear. You will make a family of your own, I promise you. It will take time, plenty of it, but we will be good." He pauses to take a breath. "No, not 'but.' 'And.' *And*, we will be good."

He pulls me away and stares into my eyes. "You *are* good."

"Okay, you two, break it off," comes Time's brash voice. "There's a joke in here about narcissism and self-love, but we won't even come here. Wait. That's not right. It's possible we meant to say 'go there.'"

Future-Me smiles at Time. "Thank you."

Time merely shrugs, then gives a deep curtsy, as they tug at the pant leg of their orange jumpsuit. "Are we good?"

I can only nod. "We sure are."

"Time to go?" Time says.

"I bet you can't get enough of my hugs." I launch myself at them, giving them another tight one. "I will miss you. You've taught me so much."

Time wraps their arms around me. "It's been mutual. Without you, we don't think we would have ever changed. But we've got one more surprise."

I pull away, staring at Future-Me, whose eyes are wide with alarm, both of us worried about this new twist. "Another one? What is it?" I ask.

"Well, with all the repair that was done on the timeline, we have found some bonus interest that has been accrued that was going to go toward the end of all time, but we can safely let everything implode at that point, because there won't be anything around anyway. So we've taken those bonus years and applied them to your lifespan. Along with your three friends. And that hamster. Mary Shelley shall officially outlive every other rodent in the known universe."

"What do you mean?" I ask.

"Well, we've added approximately . . . Hmm. Do you actually want to know how many years all of you have left to live now?"

I raise my hands to my ears. "Nope. No, don't tell me. I want to lead a life of exactly zero expectations."

Time winks at me. "That's probably wise. Well then, we guess we should get going. We'll be very busy, but we'll keep checking in on you. Making sure you don't find any other way to mess up the timeline."

"Thank you again for everything. I could not have done any of this without you."

"You did it all yourself, Hazeem. You traveled the world. You tasted all the foods. You lived."

"That's high praise coming from an eternal being."

Time grabs Future-Me's arm. "We're taking this one with us. He's very well-behaved, unlike his younger version. Well, Time shall be ever changing. Goodbye, Hazeem."

I wave to the both of them. "See you both in the future."

CHAPTER SIXTY-TWO

As I make my way back into the house, I'm filled with a calm as everyone stares at me. A sudden hushed silence diffuses through the room as if they're weighing who I am.

Whatever makes me my father's son, my grandmother's grandson.

And in this moment, I am no longer filled with emptiness. I am nearly full.

My mom looks at me with pride on her face, because I think she finally sees me for who I am. And I can decide for myself what I want to do for the rest of my life, but I know that I want everyone here to be part of it.

Especially Jack, who's already made himself known to Holly and Yamany. I wish I'd spent less time being worried and more time realizing that I'll be fine.

I am not perfect, but I am good.

I am not broken, but I am good.

I am not empty, but I am good.

And I hope for the rest of my life, I know that I will always be good.

Because I'll no longer be counting the years that pass by; I'll collect every tear and store them in a reservoir of memories.

Now that time is no longer my enemy.

But my friend.

ACKNOWLEDGMENTS

Ack!

In the words of the immortal Xiran Jay Zhao, if you're going to pirate this book, at least leave me a review!

Once again. Can't believe I'm getting another book published. How unreal, but totally real, is this?

I've got to thank Alex Borbolla—your editing insight has made this book so much better than I could've imagined it. Thank you for your patience as I worked through all our revisions together.

And to the rest of the Bloomsbury team—Kei Nakatsuka, John Candell, Oona Patrick—thank you for making this book a reality. Your hard work brings me so much joy!

To my agent, Natalie Lakosil, whatever will I do without you! Thank you for continuing to keep my spirits up and keep me going on this fight to get my words out there.

To my mom—the best I could've ever wished for. Thank you for always loving me through it all.

To my sister—how I keep annoying you, but I appreciate you for always keeping me on the straight and narrow. Or . . . at least, for always trying, lol.

To my nephew—love you to bits, and I'm glad we're finally connecting and having tons of fun together!

To Benson, every single day of this trial is made easier because you're by my side. Love you so dang much!

To Alex and Raffe—yes, you are the best doggies in the world. Thank you for always surprising me with . . . surprises, lol.

To the Naggy Shrews—always and forever. Keep nagging at me, and don't stop with the goss.

To the 99 Dead, wow how long has this journey together been? So grateful for your presence in my life.

And to all the wonderful librarians and teachers—please know I will be eternally grateful for all of you, because the work that you do in getting books to all the young people out there, is so much more important than any words we authors can put down on paper. You are the true rockstars!

To the parents of queer kids—know that your love, support, and ferocious defense of your wonderful children won't go unnoticed. They will remember every single time you stand up for them for the rest of their lives.

To every reader of this book, I hope you enjoy this story that started off from a very dark place in my life, but that has now become a torch to guide me along the way. And I hope you'll think of it as a message of hope, for when things get really difficult.

And to always remember, for everything you've put off

doing—the apologies you've held back, the dances you're waiting to have, the fatty fried foods you have to sample, the one crush you want to ask out on a date, the one book you have to finish writing—that there is . . .

No time like now.

Naz.